FISHING FOR MURDER: A 1920S HISTORICAL COZY MYSTERY

AN EVIE PARKER MYSTERY BOOK 16

SONIA PARIN

ISBN: 9798842817023

CHAPTER 1

❦

Spring, Halton House, 1922

"Come along, Holmes." Walking across the hall, Evie stepped out into the lovely spring morning and found Tom standing by his motor car, his hands in his pockets, his lips curved into a smile of blissful satisfaction as he cast an appreciative look around, no doubt taking in the fine day and perhaps even thinking about the days to come.

Despite the clear skies and bright sunshine, a chill hung in the air and they had both dressed accordingly.

Tom wore a cap and his buff colored driving coat over his dark gray suit, while Evie had opted for a lightweight yet warm woolen coat in beige, something she thought she might regret along the way as it hadn't rained in some time and the roads would no doubt be quite dusty.

Millicent, having fully embraced her new role as her secretary, hovered nearby, looking very officious as she read from her list of travel items, while Evie's new lady's maid, Merrin, confirmed the item's presence in the backseat of the motor.

As she approached, Evie met Merrin's glance. Nodding, she gave the young woman an encouraging smile.

After her brief stint in prison, Merrin Smith had arrived from London and had joined the household, stepping into her new position with wonderful ease. Although, it had taken a few days for the young woman to become accustomed to Evie employing her first name instead of her family name, as it happened in most households.

Evie smiled as she recalled hearing Millicent's explanation. *Her ladyship is rather unique. Some might say, she is unconventional, others find her quite odd. You should make up your own mind.*

After giving it some thought, Evie decided she rather liked being described as unconventional, as it released her from the usual confinements imposed by society.

Yes, indeed, she liked it very much.

Since their journey would take them all the way to the Peak District, Tom had decided to acquire a more suitable vehicle, at least, that had been his excuse for the extravagant purchase of an *Alfa Romeo RL*.

The touring motor had the benefit of being a race model, something Tom had talked about at great length and with sparkling excitement. Mostly, he had been thrilled to get his hands on one of only a handful made. The fact it had seats in the back for passengers had been a point of contention as those seats were now burdened with luggage.

Smiling at her, Tom held the passenger door open. "Are we ready?"

Evie was about to answer when a footman rushed out of the house and handed Millicent a small basket.

Inspecting the contents, Millicent gave a nod of approval and smiled at Evie. "In honor of the new motor car, milady. Cook has prepared *Cannoli* for your trip."

An Italian sweet for an Italian motor car!

"How marvelous." Evie glanced at Tom. She knew he had been feeling a great deal of trepidation and increasing concern over the amount of luggage being loaded but surely this would sweeten the deal.

Tom snorted. 'If you'd asked me what we should take on our trip, I would never have thought of taking *Cannoli*."

"I'm sure we'll appreciate it in a few hours' time when we're driving through the middle of nowhere," Evie remarked.

He patted his pockets. "Do you have everything you need?"

Evie checked her handbag. Seeing the small

revolver nestled in the bottom, she smiled and nodded. "Yes, I believe I do."

Tom lifted an eyebrow and murmured, "Countess? I thought we'd talked about this."

Evie lifted her chin, a clear indication she was prepared to launch another round of arguments to booster her reasoning.

She would not leave the revolver behind.

Recently, Evie had faced a killer who'd threatened to shoot her. The experience had made her aware of her vulnerability so she'd sworn she would be better prepared next time, and she had no doubt there would be a next time.

Acknowledging her concerns, Tom had spent the last two weeks poring through every newspaper he'd had sent to him from the Peak District, looking for any indication they might be headed for trouble. Confident they would spend a week staying near a village with no history of violence, he had tried to convince her there would be no need to take the weapon along.

However, Evie would not be swayed. "Better to be safe than sorry," she murmured.

When she didn't see Holmes standing beside her, Evie turned but instead of locating Holmes, she saw Henrietta, Sara and Toodles standing at the porticoed entrance.

They presented an unhappy portrait, something they had no doubt rehearsed for days as a protest for being left behind.

Henrietta, the Dowager Countess of Woodridge,

lifted a lace handkerchief to her eye and made a show of wiping away an imaginary tear. Sara, her mother-in-law and also the Dowager Countess of Woodridge, looked crestfallen, while her granny, Toodles, expressed her displeasure by puffing out her cheeks and lowering her brows into a deep scowl.

Tom sidled up to Evie and gave her sleeve a discreet tug. "It's emotional blackmail," he murmured. "Don't fall for it, Countess."

"Oh, Tom. I do hate to be the cause of their distress and unhappiness."

"Do not, I beg you, weaken your resolve. You know the footmen are hiding behind the doors ready for a signal from them to bring out their luggage."

Evie sighed. "You do know there is nothing preventing them from following us in the Duesenberg."

Tom grinned. "I took care of that."

"Oh, dear. What did you do?"

"I sent Edmonds on an errand. He should return later today. Far too late for them to give chase."

"I still think we're being harsh. Henrietta loves the Peak District. She has many friends there and…"

Tom lifted an eyebrow.

Evie pushed out a weary breath. "Fine, but don't blame me if they give us the silent treatment when we return."

"We seem to have differing views on the matter," he whispered. "You see their silence as punishment, whereas I see it as a blessing."

Millicent walked up to her, her notebook in hand.

"Milady, everything is in order. Do you have any last-minute instructions?"

Evie glanced at the sad trio. "You must be firm with them, Millicent. Don't let them harass you and wrestle the information out of you." Evie knew that if they discovered their destination, nothing would prevent them from following at their leisure.

Millicent's eye twitched. "I believe they already know it is quite futile to question me." She glanced at Evie's new lady's maid. "Besides, I have Merrin to help bolster my confidence."

Evie hoped that would be enough to deter the others. Turning, she called out to Holmes, "Come along, Holmes, or you'll be left behind."

The little French pug took a step forward and gave her a halfhearted wag of his tail. Looking over his shoulder, he took a step back, swung around and trotted back toward the steps.

"Holmes, what is wrong with you today?" Evie demanded.

Her butler, Edgar, sighed and stepped forward. "My lady, if I may be permitted to explain. It would appear Holmes does not wish to go."

Evie's eyebrows hitched up. "Not go?"

Edgar confirmed it with a small nod. "I'm afraid it is entirely my fault, my lady."

"Edgar, whatever do you mean?"

Her butler lowered his gaze and sighed. "Last week, whilst taking our morning constitutional, we ventured further afield than we normally do and… Well, Holmes met a friend. Her name is Miss Penelope."

"Oh, I didn't realize we had a new neighbor." She turned to Millicent. "Please remind me to stop by and introduce myself."

Edgar cleared his throat again. "I'm afraid there's been a misunderstanding, my lady. Miss Penelope is a French pug. Holmes is rather taken with her and he clearly does not wish to be parted."

Holmes… In love?

"Countess." Tom gave his watch a tap.

"Tom, can you believe this? Holmes doesn't wish to come with us." Evie sighed. "I suppose I should say goodbye."

"Countess, you can wave goodbye from the car." As they made their way to the motor, he hurried her along, issuing further warnings, "Don't look back. You'll only encourage them."

Settling into her seat, Evie pushed out a breath. "This is all very odd. Holmes doesn't wish to join us and the others are doing their utmost to change our minds. I do feel we are being unfair. It's not as if they would get underfoot. They are quite capable of entertaining themselves.'

Tom went through the motions of starting the car. As he sat back and smiled with appreciation at the sound of the engine, he said, "That's just it. We want an uneventful week. Fishing is a quiet, contemplative sport."

"Tom, anyone who heard you speak would think the dowagers and Toodles are magnets for trouble."

He snorted. "You never heard me say that but, you must admit, they have caught a whiff of excitement and I fear they are now quite addicted to the thrill of the chase. To their credit, they seem to excel at it, but this is a quiet vacation."

Evie pressed her lips together to stop herself from reminding him she'd wanted to get some target practice. Not exactly a quiet pursuit, she thought.

"Smile and wave," he said as he got them on their way.

Evie looked out the passenger window. Holmes had positioned himself behind Edgar's leg and peered out at her while the dowagers and Toodles were leaning into each other as if seeking comfort and solace.

"Good heavens, they're trying to squeeze every last ounce of sympathy."

"Save your sympathy for Millicent," Tom suggested. "She's already developed a nervous twitch."

Evie settled back and folded her arms. She'd been looking forward to their adventure and seeing the countryside from the vantage point of a motor instead of a train. However, now she would have to devote some time to thinking about making reparations. Heavens, they hadn't even told them about Tom's impending knighthood, something else they had kept hidden from them.

"Did you bring your Brownie camera?" she asked.

Tom nodded. "I hope you're not looking for excuses

to turn back and delay our departure. Or, heaven forbid, cancel it."

"Tom! I wouldn't dream of it. This is as much my vacation as it is yours."

Two weeks of nothing but peace and quiet.

CHAPTER 2

❦

*B*reaking down their journey to manageable distances had allowed Evie and Tom to indulge in every delight offered by the small villages along the way.

Over the last three days, they had stayed at two quaint inns, enjoying luncheon and dinner in various village pubs.

Unencumbered by time constraints, they had explored country laneways and winding narrow streets at leisure, taking in the backdrop views of lush green hills and valleys—not once feeling they needed to rush anywhere.

"How exactly are you going to explain this?" Tom asked as Evie posed in front of yet another village pub.

"I don't know what you mean." Evie adjusted her hat and gave it a slight tilt. "Make sure you capture the sign in the photograph, please."

"Most of the photographs I've taken are of you

standing outside a pub. They'll think I've led you along the road to ruination."

"Nonsense. Everything is so wonderfully picturesque and the country inns delightful and quaint. I would hate to return without a single keepsake of our journey."

"Countess, you have dozens of them."

"Well, Tom... I'm sure that in years to come we'll appreciate the photographs and the memories they captured."

"I'll be too busy taking more photographs of you." He shook his head. "Smile and hold still." He turned the winding knob on his camera and looked up. "All done. Ready to move on?" Checking his watch, he nodded, "We should be able to arrive at Bamford by mid-afternoon. From there, it will be a short drive to our final destination."

Evie looked away and winced. While they'd had a lengthy luncheon, it hadn't been enough time to recover from the long stretch of road they had trekked across. Not even Tom's competent driving or luxurious vehicle had spared her the discomfort of the many bumpy roads they had traversed. "I wouldn't mind stretching my legs first."

They meandered along the main street up to the corner where Tom signaled to the side street. "I believe what you are looking for is this way."

"How do you know what I'm looking for? Are you about to tell me I'm predictable?"

"Every stop we have made along the way has

included a visit to the local cemetery." He smiled. "Of course, if I'm wrong, we could head the other way."

Evie lifted her chin. "We're already headed this way. Let's see where the street takes us."

Tom feigned surprise. "Oh, look, there's the village church and the cemetery. I'm actually surprised you haven't suggested taking photographs of the gravestones."

"That would be bizarre, I'm sure."

They walked on at leisure. As they reached the church, Evie narrowed her eyes. Then, she slowed down and finally stopped.

"Has your enthusiasm waned?" Tom asked.

"Not at all, but I can see there's a service in progress. I wouldn't want to intrude."

Tom joined her in narrowing his eyes. "By the looks of it, we wouldn't be. On the contrary, our presence would most likely be welcomed."

They stopped at the gates to the church and decided not to go any further. The funeral service appeared to be nearing the end.

"How odd. There's only one mourner but an abundance of flowers," Evie murmured.

"Perhaps the deceased only knew one person in the village," Tom suggested.

"That's a possibility. Their friends must live very far away and she or he might have been a recent arrival in the village."

When the service ended, the vicar had a brief word

with the mourner, then left the woman to say her final farewells.

She did not linger.

Turning, she walked away only to stop. She turned and spent a brief moment looking back.

"Regret?" Evie murmured.

"What was that?" Tom asked.

"I'm trying to interpret the gesture. Did you notice the way she looked back? It was only brief, but the look felt full of regret. Perhaps the deceased was only young."

"I take it we'll be having a closer look? Your curiosity has obviously been piqued."

Evie thought there wouldn't be any point since there wasn't a headstone to provide even the most basic information such as the person's name and date of birth. "We'd have better luck with an obituary posted in the newspaper. There must be one." Evie sighed and looked around the graveyard. "Then again, we are on vacation and I'd rather avoid all talk of death."

"I'm sure it won't hurt to have a quick look. You are clearly intrigued." Tom cupped her elbow and led her through the gate.

"Have you ever experienced a moment of curiosity and have had to settle for filling in the gaps yourself?" Evie asked.

"I can't say that I have," he mused.

Of course, he was quite right. She was curious but

she feared she'd have to settle for whatever they could imagine.

Two men stood at the edge of the cemetery. They both wore ragged looking coats and caps. One stood leaning against a shovel, while the other stood with his hands in his pockets, and a cigarette dangling from the corner of his mouth.

"Tuberoses and snowdrops," Evie whispered as she glanced at the bouquets of flowers surrounding the grave.

"Is that unusual?" Tom asked.

"Not necessarily, but it is rather odd. Perhaps those were the only flowers available." Evie shrugged. "I suppose I shall have to contend myself with assuming the deceased favored those flowers."

He pointed to one and said, "That bouquet is the only one with a card."

Evie leaned down and read it.

You will be missed.

The words echoed in her mind. She wondered if the note had been written by the single mourner who had been present or by someone who hadn't been able to attend.

"You're puzzling over this." Tom looked around the graveyard. "I could approach those two fellows over there. They might know something."

"Tom, that would be taking our curiosity too far. How would you explain it?"

"I doubt they'd mind me asking. They've been glancing our way. I believe they are just as curious as we are." He gave a firm nod and headed in their direction.

While Tom walked toward the two men, Evie remained standing by the grave. She assumed the two men would be moving in soon to complete the process of internment. The fact they hadn't already suggested they might be giving two late comers the opportunity to pay their final respects.

Tom had been right in pointing out her interest in visiting the local churches they had come across. Most villages had been quite small, some with only a dozen or so houses, an inn and a couple of stores, all surrounded by farms and farm houses.

She cast her gaze around the graveyard and saw at least a half dozen headstones that looked no older than a couple of years. No moss had managed to gather around them and the names had not yet begun to erode.

Evie couldn't really explain her interest. Was it idle curiosity? She could claim she was equally interested in seeing how many people they encountered at the local inns.

In reality, she still felt the rumbling echoes of the last few years. The senseless loss of lives cut short by either the war or the Spanish flu that had trailed on its wake.

There was already talk of the lost generation. Of women who would never marry simply because there were not enough men to meet the demands. Those who had perished were not the only ones who had been deprived of a future. The ones who remained, the survivors, had now been denied the choice of a full life.

She heard footsteps crunching on loose gravel and turned. Tom had his eyes to the ground and she could see the two men walking toward the open grave, ready to complete their task.

"Her name was Enid Carlton and quite new to the village," he said when he reached her. "You were right on that score."

That still didn't explain the attendance of a single mourner. Had she not made friends in the village since her arrival?

"Heavens, how new was she to the village?"

Tom cupped her elbow. As they walked toward the gate, he said, "She moved here two weeks ago after inheriting her great aunt's house a couple of streets away from here. The woman we saw attending the service was her maid, Alice Breer."

A cloud appeared from out of nowhere and covered the sun. It was enough to make Evie shiver.

Enid Carlton.

Had moving to this village been a new start for her? Had her death been sudden, catching her in the middle of fulfilling a dream?

Giving a small nod, Evie said, "I suppose we should make a start. We don't want to arrive at an awkward time."

Frowning, Tom asked, "Awkward? We've stayed at houses were guests have staggered in at all hours."

"Ignore what I said. I'm just prattling." Evie knew

she wanted to rein in her curiosity and ignore everything that threatened to distract her from having a pleasant time.

They returned to the inn with the intention of collecting their luggage. Unfortunately, along the way, they crossed paths with Alice Breer, the woman who had been at the funeral service.

Evie recognized the blue scarf she wore as well as her upright manner which appeared to be almost exaggerated.

When she glanced at them, the woman responded to Evie's smile with a small nod. She carried a parcel tied with string and, despite only catching the briefest glimpse, Evie managed to see a postmark suggesting she had just been to the post office.

They continued walking toward the pub, their silence broken when Evie asked, "Did they know how she died?"

Tom adjusted the strap of his Brownie camera on his shoulder and nodded. "She died in her sleep. It was rather sudden and quite unexpected."

Evie tried to remember if he had mentioned the woman's age. "She must have been very old."

"Not at all. In fact, they made a point of lamenting the fact she had been so young."

"Oh, I see. Perhaps she had a condition and the local doctor had not been aware of it."

You will be missed…

Who would write such a message and not bother attending the service?

How had the people who'd sent flowers found out about the death?

Someone must have contacted Enid Carlton's friends and acquaintances, as well as family, of course.

But why had they not attended?

They arrived at the pub and, stepping inside, Evie decided to dismiss all her thoughts of the young woman before they nestled in her mind and completely took over.

Their suitcases had already been brought down and put away in the manager's office.

Tom settled the account and a young man helped him load the luggage into the motor car.

"Ready?"

Evie looked down the main street toward the corner leading to the church. For the briefest moment, she felt a strong tug urging her to return and, perhaps even go beyond and straight to the young woman's house to talk with the maid.

Pushing out a breath, she nodded.

Tom held the passenger door open and Evie settled into her seat, her attention fixed on straightening her skirt and coat. She continued to fiddle with her clothes until Tom settled beside her.

Tipping his hat back, he asked, "Are we still curious or are you ready to leave?"

"You must agree, it was rather interesting." She gave a small nod. "I believe that was a fine way to hone our observations skills."

"Observation and, perhaps, our creativity?"

"Yes, that too. It never hurts to stretch the mind." In the past, Evie thought, they had employed the tactic to imagine connections between separate events.

She really couldn't see any reason to linger. Evie gave him a wide smile. Besides, she wouldn't dream of ruining his fishing vacation. "Drive on, please."

Tom studied her for a moment before handing her a copy of a local newspaper. "I thought you might like to entertain yourself."

Evie took the newspaper but did not look at it. "Thank you but I'm sure the scenery will keep my attention engaged."

CHAPTER 3

Allenford Castle
The Earl of Moorsley's estate

With the exception of two stops to admire the Derwent River, which wove its way along the Peak District, Evie and Tom focused on arriving at their host's home in time to avoid disrupting afternoon tea.

"The river actually cuts through the estate," Evie remarked. "And I believe the lodge we'll be staying at is right on its banks. Just think of it, you'll only need to walk several paces to cast your line."

"That's rather inconvenient. I was hoping to be able to cast my line from a window." Tom glanced at Evie and beamed a smile at her.

"I suppose we can't have everything all of the time."

Evie clasped her hands on her lap and frowned. "I really don't understand why Holmes refused to come with us. He doesn't seem to understand the concept of being a companion. I miss not having him on my lap." Right that moment, she would have found the distraction comforting.

"How quickly they grow up," Tom remarked as he changed gears and swept them up a slight incline.

When they reached the top, they had an uninterrupted view of the castle and the surrounding landscape.

Tom slowed down to take in the sight. "I'm not sure I would call that a castle. I'm actually disappointed."

"If you look closely, you'll see the turret at the end of one wing."

"Only one turret?" He shook his head. "My expectations have been shattered."

They found the entrance to the estate and slowed down when a man emerged from the small gatekeeper's house.

Recognizing the elderly man, Evie greeted him by name, "Benjamin."

To his credit, the gatekeeper remembered Evie. Giving her a welcoming smile, he waved them through, directing them to follow the treelined road.

As they approached, they saw a number of motor cars lined near the entrance, a gardener disappearing around a corner, his rake slung over his shoulder. Evie didn't see any tire marks on the gravel around the entrance so she assumed he had just finished tidying up.

"I imagine they have just returned from a day's fishing. Lord Moorsley's estate offers one of the prime spots for the sport."

Tom leaned in slightly and smiled. "I'm impressed, Countess. You have managed to remain convincingly enthusiastic throughout the entire trip."

Evie lifted her chin. "I don't know what you mean."

"Admit it. You agreed to this only because you think this is what I want."

"Well, isn't it?" When he didn't respond, Evie frowned. "Tom Winchester, say you wanted to come fishing right this minute."

Tom chuckled. "I might have mentioned it in passing."

"Yes, but did you mean it? Actually, now that I think about it, I don't know why I indulged you."

"Are you admitting to doing this simply because you thought it's what I wanted and needed?"

Thinking about their day to day lives, Evie often wondered how he felt about being surrounded by so many women. Unlike the average peer or well-to-do gentleman, Tom didn't belong to any of the many gentlemen's clubs. To be fair to him, he didn't seem to need the company of other men and he never even bothered to escape from the occasional upheaval at Halton House by seeking solitude.

"I assumed you would enjoy it." Evie shifted. "As a matter of fact, I rather enjoy fishing. As a child, I was encouraged to pursue productive activities. Fishing happened to be one of them. My parents wished to instil in us a sense of value and appreciation for the simple pleasures in life."

"And did you eat the product of your labors?"

Evie grinned. "No, we used to sell our catch to neighbors and spend the proceeds on sweets."

"How very enterprising of you. Perhaps that was the whole purpose of the exercise."

"Yes, I believe you're right. My brother would only eat half his sweets and keep the rest for the moment when I craved a sweet and he would sell them to me for a profit. I'm not surprised he grew up to make his own fortune. I believe your funds are in good hands."

"I'm glad to know I'll able to keep you in the manner to which you've become accustomed."

"I suspect there is a double entendre hidden some-where in that remark. Let me warn you, I will not fish for my supper."

A butler emerged and stood on the top step of the entrance. When Tom brought the motor to a stop, the butler hurried down the stone steps, with two footmen following close behind.

"No matter how many times I witness this, I remain impressed by such attention, especially in the wilds of the Peak District," Tom remarked.

"The wilds of the Peak District?" Evie smiled. "Some of the grandest estates are found in this area. Chatsworth being the largest."

A footman held the door open for Tom. Before Tom

could button his coat and walk around to help Evie step down, another footman hurried to open Evie's passenger door.

Evie joined Tom and they both stood looking at the magnificent stone building with its many mullioned windows glinting in the sun.

The butler inclined his head, "Lady Woodridge. Mr. Winchester. Welcome to Allenford Castle."

Evie gave him a warm smile. She remembered the butler from her last visit a number of years before and knew him to be quite amiable. "Simmons. What a lovely day to arrive. The weather has rolled out a welcoming carpet for us."

Turning toward the entrance, Evie saw a man dressed in country tweeds approaching them. As tall as Tom but quite a few years older, he walked at a brisk pace, his head held high.

Even before reaching them, he called out, "Lady Woodridge. It has been too long."

Had it? Evie couldn't remember exactly how long it had been. She only knew Allenford Castle had been one of many houses in the area she had visited with her husband during their numerous tours of the area.

"May I present Tom Winchester. Tom, this is the Earl of Moorsley."

The Earl of Moorsley extended his hand and proceeded to speak at a fast clip, "Moorsley will do. Although, you'll hear most of the guests calling me Brigadier. Feel free to do so. I'm afraid I have rather bad news. The lodge is leaking."

"Oh, dear." Evie wasn't entirely sure what that meant.

The Brigadier went on to explain, "A few days ago, the roof suffered some wind damage and the rain did the rest. The weather's cleared now but, I daresay, you wouldn't want to risk it. You could still make a day of it there. You'll find most guests will disperse straight after breakfast. Simmons can organize a basket to take with you or my man Graham could bring it to you. Man of few words. Speaks only when he needs to. He knows the river inside and out and can show you all the best spots."

"That would be lovely, Brigadier. I had promised Tom some quiet time."

"Then, it's settled. Simmons has already organized some rooms for you here. You'll be very comfortable."

Evie didn't need the assurance as she still remembered the sumptuous rooms in the castle. "That's very gracious, Brigadier."

"You're our guests, whether you stay at the lodge or at the house." He gestured to the motor cars. "We have a small group. They've been here for a couple of days and a few stragglers will arrive in the next few days. Once they see the river, they always stop for a spot of fishing along the way. In fact, they usually stop several times until they finally arrive here. Terribly unsporting of them, if you ask me. I know what they're up to, trying to get a head start and probably joking about draining the river of fish before the little swimmers can reach us." He cocked an eyebrow at Tom who immediately raised both hands, palms up as if to dissuade the Brigadier of the suspicion. No, indeed, they had not stopped to fish. "Come in. Afternoon tea will be served shortly. That'll give you just enough time to settle in." He turned to Tom. "Did you bring your rods? Never mind if you didn't. We have plenty. Simmons will take care of you." He nodded. "I'll see you shortly."

Lord Moorsley swung away and, walking in the officious manner he was known for, he marched up the steps while Evie and Tom followed at leisure.

Evie smiled at Tom. "I meant to warn you. The Brigadier enjoys drawing a full picture. It's not enough to say there are guests here, he feels you should also know there are more guests arriving, if only they would pull themselves away from the urge to stop for a spot of fishing along the way."

Tom leaned in and remarked, "Countess, you might be in for a dull time."

"What do you mean?"

"Did you see the number of cars. There'll be as many men, if not more. You'll probably be the only lady present."

Evie smiled. "You'd be surprised." In time, Evie thought, Tom would come to realize no sporting activity or any type of social gathering was ever without the presence of ladies.

Catching the glint of amusement in her eyes, Tom asked, "What did I miss?"

"Look at that splendid staircase," Evie said as they

entered the hall. The stone steps curved up to the next level and were wide enough to allow at least four people to climb up without needing to tuck their elbows in.

A woman dressed in a stylish tweed suit was making her way up the stairs, her steps slow, almost pensive. For a moment, Evie found herself wondering what thoughts she might be entertaining.

Did I make the right decision in coming here?

Is this going to be another wasted weekend?

I had options...

Evie smiled.

I should put back the little trinket I took. What do I want with a snuff box? I'm sure someone will eventually notice it missing...

He said he would be here. Did he lie? Is he interested in someone else...

"I suspect there are more than a few eligible gentlemen present." Evie murmured.

"I see," Tom nodded, "and as many ladies eager to entice them. Is that what you're implying?"

"Actually," Evie tilted her head, "don't be surprised to find their baskets brimming with the day's catch. Women can be surprisingly enthusiastic about fishing."

As Evie turned to smile at Tom, her gaze fell on a table displaying a large vase of flowers.

Snowdrops and tuberoses.

Stilling, she stared at them, her eyes not blinking.

After what seemed like an eternity, she tried to reason with herself, saying they were in season and, quite possibly, taking pride of place in more than a few households.

This was nothing but a coincidence.

Shaking her head, she decided she wouldn't mention the flowers.

CHAPTER 4

❦

A footman showed Evie through to her
sumptuously appointed room. It came as no
surprise to find a large four poster bed, tapestries of
hunting scenes on the walls and a door leading to a
petit boudoir, all quite typical in such houses that had
been standing for over a hundred years.

When she glanced out the window, Evie brightened
with delight as she caught a glint of the river winding
its way across the estate.

Despite what Tom might think, she did enjoy traveling around the countryside and taking part in the
calendar of annual activities. It was all about making
connections and keeping them. Of course, there was
also the entertainment value. Everyone seemed to
know everyone or they were usually fast on their way
to doing so.

Back home, in her earlier years, there had been the
house on Fifth Avenue facing the park and the summer

cottage in Rhode Island. The time spent there had always been her favorite. Away from prying eyes, she had been allowed more freedoms, at least, the type of freedoms she enjoyed whilst away from prying parental eyes. Such simple things as walking barefoot along creeks and the beach and getting into playful scuffles with her brother or local children. Unlike other parents who were strict about only meeting the right people, her parents were not particularly keen to subject her friends to serious vetting. She could come and go as she pleased and meet whomever she wanted.

In a few years, young Seth, her charge and current Earl of Woodridge, would be introduced into society and she wished him to mirror her childhood by also experiencing life outside of his social circle. Yes, indeed, she wished to nurture and guide him into becoming a well-rounded young man.

Losing her train of thought for a moment, she had to remind herself these social events were all part and parcel of being responsible for someone else. She needed to maintain the connections for Seth's benefit.

The edge of her lips kicked up. Despite losing his parents at a young age, Seth was a lucky little boy. He had Tom and Millicent to balance out the strict regimental upbringing imposed on him during his formative years and she had no doubt that would make a world of difference in his future life.

As she waited for her luggage to be brought in, she relieved herself of her dusty traveling coat and took a moment to empty her mind and appreciate the view.

The fact she had arrived without a lady's maid did not go unnoticed. Soon after the luggage was brought in and she changed into her fresh clothes, Evie heard a light knock at the door.

A young maid walked in, dropped a curtsy, and introduced herself. "I'm Barclay, milady. When Lady Moorsley heard you'd arrived, she sent me directly to assist you." Her eyes strayed to the luggage.

Evie interpreted the deep swallow she took as possible concern over her tardiness in arriving.

Smiling, Evie asked, "What's your Christian name?"

"Rose, milady."

"Would you mind if I call you Rose?"

The young woman looked surprised. "If you wish."

"Thank you and as for Lady Moorsley's offer, it's very kind, but I'm sure I can manage."

Rose gave a fierce shake of her head. "Oh, no, milady. Lady Moorsley wouldn't hear of it."

Belatedly, Evie remembered Lady Moorsley did not care to concern herself with unnecessary problems. If she went to the trouble of deciding something, she liked it to be followed to the letter. Evie assumed Rose would rather avoid crossing her. "Very well."

Rose proceeded to unpack Evie's suitcases, along the way murmuring her admiration for the tidy packing.

"All credit must go my new lady's maid, Merrin."

"There's hardly a crease in these blouses."

"I'll be sure to mention it." Evie sat at the dresser

and fussed with her hair. "Do you know how many other ladies are present?"

"They come and go, milady. Yesterday there were ten. Nine left and only one remained. Today, four more arrived and now there are five. The new guests arrived this morning and look set to spend a few days here."

Only five? That meant most of the gentlemen were married but had traveled without their wives who had possibly chosen to pursue other interests.

Rose held up two dresses. "Which would you prefer to wear this evening, milady?"

Not used to being offered a choice since Millicent had always known best, Evie left it up to Rose. "Surprise me." A glance at the reflection in the mirror told her the maid had once again been taken by surprise.

Evie abandoned her efforts to make her hair look straight, and stood up. Glancing at the dress Rose had selected, she smiled. "Very good choice, thank you, Rose."

"The dressing gong is rung promptly at five, milady."

Thanking her again, Evie made her way down. At least, that was her intention.

Allenford Castle had vast corridors stretching the length and breadth of the building and held the largest collection of armors, tapestries and paintings Evie had ever seen.

There were two long galleries. One faced the front of the property while the other faced the back. Between them, there was a large courtyard.

Views of the surrounding landscape could be admired from the many mullioned windows on one side, while the opposite wall was lined with portraits going back to Elizabethan times.

Although tempted to reacquaint herself with both galleries, Evie was eager to find Tom and join their host. While the Brigadier's gatherings were always relaxed, it would be bad form to wander off without first making an appearance.

She headed for the stairs and found her steps slowing as she remembered the display of flowers she had seen in the hall. "Tuberoses and snowdrops are spring blooms," she reminded herself. Why should she find it strange to see them on display? There were masses of them planted around her own gardens at Halton House as well as throughout the countryside.

Drawing in a long breath, she once again made a conscious decision. She would not mention the flowers. At least, not until she had a reasonable excuse to do so.

A door opened and closed. Evie turned and saw Tom approaching, his eyes bouncing from one painting to the next.

Seeing her, he smiled. "Countess."

"Tom, I can't believe I'm the first one down."

"You're not down just yet."

"Oh, I would have been if I hadn't lingered. There are two long galleries we should look at. The paintings are magnificent. Do please remind me."

"Is that the only reason you lingered?"

Evie felt her cheeks coloring. "Whatever do you mean?"

Shrugging, he gave her his arm and they made their way down the stairs. When they reached the bottom, he asked, "Which way? Follow the footman with the tray? Or do you wish to discuss the tuberoses and snowdrops?"

Evie's lips parted. She drew in a sharp breath and released it full of indignation. "You noticed and you didn't say anything."

"Nor did you." He grinned. "What am I to make of that?"

Shrugging, Evie said, "I wanted to avoid making a fuss over nothing. You must admit, there is nothing unusual about the combination."

"And yet here we are, standing at the foot of the stairs, both doing our very best to not look at the arrangement of blooms." His eyes twinkled. "Shall we take a peek?"

"Tom, you mustn't tease. I've spent the last half hour doing battle with my conscience. This fishing trip is all about you and here I am entertaining suspicions just because we came across a funeral service with only one mourner."

"A single mourner and an abundance of tuberoses and snowdrops. Don't forget those." He looked up and saw another footman carrying a tray. He disappeared through a set of double doors while another emerged with an empty tray. "If we don't decide soon, we'll miss out on your favorite cucumber sandwiches. Do the flowers carry some significance or not?"

Without giving it any thought, Evie answered in the affirmative. Yes, indeed, they had to.

"Countess?"

"Yes. I believe they do." Her shoulders lowered and she felt a sense of instant relief. Not only had she been obsessing about the flowers, she had also spent a great deal of energy trying to convince herself there was no reason to find anything suspicious about them.

"Lady Woodridge."

Evie and Tom turned and saw a woman coming down the stairs.

Evie recognized her immediately. She walked with the confidence and ease of someone who knew her place in life.

Gracelyn, the Brigadier's wife.

Her smile sparkled in her eyes and Evie remembered her as someone who found joy in everything she did.

Despite not having seen her in more than five years, the only change Evie noticed was her hair, which had been styled in the latest fashion.

"Lady Moorsley." Lowering her voice, she murmured, "It's the Brigadier's wife."

"Gracelyn, please," Lady Moorsley said as she reached the bottom of the stairs. She gave them a bright smile and before Evie could make the introductions, she turned to Tom. "You must be Tom

Winchester. How delightful to finally meet you. And, yes, I have heard a great deal about you."

"Lady Moorsley."

"Gracelyn, please." Lady Moorsley winked at Evie. "The first time I met Evie, it was all I heard from her as everyone addressed her as Lady Woodridge and she insisted on being, in her own words, plain Evie." She clasped her hands. "Now, what are you two doing lingering in the hall?"

"We're admiring your blooms," Tom admitted.

"Which ones? At this time of the year, the house is filled with them."

"The snowdrops and tuberoses," Evie answered.

Lady Moorsley cast her gaze around the hall. When she saw them, she seemed to be taken aback. "I must admit, I hadn't noticed them. They must have just been placed there today. Although, I can't think why. We've never had plain white arrangements. Well, except for weddings or funerals, of course." Dismissing them as an oddity, she spread her hands out and herded them toward the drawing room. "Shall we?"

They walked through a set of large carved doors and found the guests spread out around the spacious drawing room, chatting and drinking tea.

Evie found the drawing room as impressive as the first time she had seen it. She knew it had once served as a ballroom and continued to do so for special occasions. The floor to ceiling windows were flanked by red velvet curtains. A massive chandelier hung in the middle with two other smaller ones at either end.

Sweeping her gaze around, Evie saw a group of men standing at the end of the drawing room, almost as if they had deliberately sought to distance themselves from everyone else. To her surprise, she didn't recognize any of them and, even if she'd known them, she thought she might have struggled to identify them unless she moved closer.

She hoped the new faces would offer a distraction from her current preoccupation. Unfortunately, her thoughts strayed back to her hostess. If she found Gracelyn's reaction to the presence of the flowers odd, she did not mention it. At least, not until the thought had settled in her mind and she could make some sense of it.

She should not have been surprised to learn Tom had also noticed them. It seemed odd that he hadn't mentioned them at first. He had either assumed she had noticed them or he had simply decided they were not worth mentioning. Then again, he must have made some sort of connection because, in the end, he had shared his observation...

Perhaps she had underestimated Tom's penchant for teasing her.

Out of the corner of her eye, she caught a movement. Turning slightly, she saw the Brigadier standing near the fireplace chatting with a group of men. He was casting an imaginary line and appeared to be sharing the triumphs of that day's fishing as he mimicked a struggle followed by a triumphant tug on said imaginary line.

"You should prepare yourselves to hear nothing but talk about fishing," Lady Moorsley warned. "Admittedly and, in case you have forgotten, the tales become more extravagant and amusing as the night wears on. So you should, at least, find them amusing. Have you fished in these parts, Tom?"

"No, it's my first time here."

"And how is your enthusiasm for the sport?"

Waning by the minute, Evie thought as she read his expression. If she had to guess, she'd say his thoughts were still entertaining questions about the flowers.

"As good as ever," he said. "I'm keen to get out there and cast a line."

Lady Moorsley gestured toward a table laden with platters of sandwiches and cake.

"Simmons," she said, drawing the attention of the butler who stood at one end.

"My lady."

"Do you happen to know where those tuberoses and snowdrops came from?" When the butler did not provide a brisk response, she added, "They are out in the hall."

"I assumed they'd been placed there under your direction, my lady."

"So you did notice them."

He nodded.

"How odd." Her attention shifted to a newcomer. "Oh, here comes Horacia Deblin. You must meet her. She is absolutely fascinating. Or, at least, I think so. She insists she's rather dull."

A woman about Evie's age walked in and headed toward them. Slim and tall, she wore the obligatory tweed jacket but had matched it with wide legged trousers. Moving with purpose, she acknowledged them with a nod and waved to someone as she strode past them.

"I lost track of time," Horacia Deblin said. "It must be all the fresh air." Shuddering, she added, "I'm not sure how I'll ever be able to return to my dismal quarters in town."

"No one is forcing you to live in squalor, my dear." Lady Moorsley turned to Evie and Tom and made the introductions. "Horacia has been cloistered in a dusty library all winter. She is one of these new breeds of women, determined to make her own way in the world and, not only that, she is actually succeeding and making her mark."

"Gracelyn, I wouldn't go so far as to make such a claim."

Lady Moorsley waved her hand in a dismissive gesture. "Oh, you are too modest. I wonder how many more generations it will take for women to abandon that silly habit?"

Evie found herself agreeing. In her opinion, women were far too modest. "What is it that you do?"

"I am writing a biography of Eleanor of Aquitaine."

"An authoritative one, I'm sure. Horacia is a graduate of Bramswood Academy." Lady Moorsley smiled at Horacia. "Who needs Oxford when you have Anita May Connors."

Without being told anything about the woman, Evie decided she had to be quite exceptional.

"Do help yourselves to some tea and sandwiches," Lady Moorsley encouraged. "If you'll excuse me, I need to circulate."

Evie put aside all thoughts of tuberoses and snow-drops and decided to focus on enjoying her stay at Allenford Castle.

As they moved toward the table, Tom asked, "Do you have a publisher already interested in your work?"

"For a book about a woman?" Horacia laughed, "I think not." Helping herself to some tea, she then turned to Evie. "I've heard stories about you, Lady Woodridge. I hope you are taking notes. Sometime, in the near or distant future, you might wish to write a memoir."

Good heavens. What an idea. Her life in black and white for all to read about. "It would read like a work of fiction," Evie assured her.

CHAPTER 5

istracted by something Horacia Deblin said, Evie only saw a blur as one of the guests swept past Tom and took him away to join a group of gentlemen discussing river currents and fly fishing.

That left Evie alone with Horacia Deblin and she seemed intent on finding out everything she could about Evie's adventures in the world of criminal activity.

"I find it all fascinating. It's not exactly the type of excitement titled ladies find the time for. You must have an inquiring mind."

Evie didn't wait for Horacia to ask if boredom with her life had led her to seek such excitement. She hurried to say, "Tom and I just happened to be in the right place at the wrong time, at least, from the criminal's perspective, it must have been the wrong time."

"And you say you consult with a Scotland Yard inspector? That's very open-minded of him."

Evie gave a small shrug. "The times are changing. To our credit, we have shown ourselves to be quite helpful."

"I'm sure that wasn't the case at first," Horacia said.

"True. We did have to prove ourselves. It's strange because Tom and I didn't actually set out to become involved in an investigation. In any case, we always try to remain in the background. After all, the police have a job to do."

"That's very accommodating of you. I'm sure you offer your own brand of enlightenment which, in turn, helps the police expedite matters," Horacia said as they were joined by another guest eager to make Evie's acquaintance.

Evie didn't notice any particular reason why Horacia would chose that moment to move away but, to Evie's dismay, Horacia Deblin did just that. She made her excuses and strayed away.

Lucian Gregson, a local landowner and regular guest at the castle had also heard about her reputation and was eager to discuss the curious goings on around his farm. Evie only heard half the conversation about animals going missing and being replaced by other animals. As she listened, her attention was pulled away by the glances she caught from Lady Moorsley and Horacia.

Had Horacia moved away to seek counsel from her friend or to share her first impressions about her?

Every time Evie looked in their direction, she caught one or the other looking back at her.

"It's almost as if the thief suffers from bouts of guilt," Lucian Gregson said. "One day I find several chickens missing and the next day, there's a new pig in the pen. What do you make of that, Lady Woodridge?"

"I really couldn't say."

"I've asked around to see if it's happening to anyone else, but I seem to be the only one graced by a bartering thief. Don't get me wrong, I'm by no means put out. Mostly, I seem to be doing quite well out of the thieving. In fact, at this rate, it would be silly of me to intervene and ruin the whole process. That pig was quite succulent."

"If you're really keen to find out the identity of the thief, you might want to set a trap," Evie suggested.

He considered the idea. "I'm not sure I have it in me. I'd be riddled with guilt. He seems to have a good system in place and I'd hate to disrupt it." Lucien Gregson finished his tea and set the cup down. "It's the strangest thing. We deal rather harshly with poachers, but this fellow seems to be fair-minded. Yes, indeed, it would be almost a shame to put an end to it all." Lucian Gregson smiled at Evie. "Thank you, Lady Woodridge."

"You're very welcome but I'm not sure I said anything of value."

"On the contrary. I needed to talk it through." He nodded. "Yes, yes, indeed."

Turning, Evie saw Tom trying to step away and extricate himself from the group of fishing enthusiasts only to be drawn into another discussion. That left her with no choice but to express an interest in someone else.

Ordinarily, she had no trouble making the rounds in a soirée and engaging anyone and everyone in conversation, but the tuberoses and snowdrops wove into her mind and took up residence... again.

Setting her teacup down, she picked up a cucumber sandwich and devoted her entire focus to nibbling it. As she did, she strolled around the drawing room, admiring the many decorative pieces on display.

A grouping of photographs caught her eye.

The images were mostly of fishing and hunting trophies. Even as she studied the photographs with interest, her mind tried to find a solution for her fixation.

Tuberoses.

Snowdrops.

Tuberoses and snowdrops...

There had to be a reason why the funeral service with a single mourner and dozens of flower arrangements had caught her attention.

Maybe her observation had nothing to do with the flowers.

Maybe it had to do with something else and she only needed to identify it. Of course, at some point, she would be willing to accept that this was nothing more than mere curiosity over a simple choice of flowers.

Evie pushed out a breath filled with frustration. She couldn't dismiss her curiosity, not after seeing yet another bunch of the same flowers. Even if it was a seasonal coincidence.

Shadowing.

The prompt emerged from out of nowhere.

She wondered if her mind was trying to offer a distraction. Recently, she had spoken with Lotte Mannering, the lady detective, and they had discussed the practice of shadowing employed in detective work.

As she continued to entertain the thought, she began to see a valid reason for it.

Shadowing required a great deal of patience and perseverance but the tactic was well worth the trouble and, indeed, essential as it often yielded surprising results.

First, however, one needed a suspect or person of interest and Evie didn't have one because, in reality, there was no crime that she could see.

Not yet, she thought.

In the past, she had encountered bizarre circum-stances and witnessed the oddest behavior which had led her and Tom to discover and investigate several crimes.

Giving herself an encouraging nod, Evie decided it would be best to forge ahead with her suspicions, such as they were.

She could only keep her eyes open and observe people's behavior or notice things that appeared to be unusual, such as the flower arrangements of tuberoses and snowdrops, she insisted.

"Always keep a look out for telltale signs," Evie

whispered as she picked up a photograph. Studying it, she tried to determine when the photograph had been taken.

The Gibson girl hairstyle, Evie thought, with large volumes of hair gathered at the top had been popular in the Edwardian era.

The young woman in the photograph stood next to another woman, possibly twenty years older. Evie didn't see any similarities in appearance so she didn't think they were related.

On closer inspection, Evie noticed the aquiline nose on the young woman and identified her as Gracelyn, Lady Moorsley.

"And who's the other woman?" Evie whispered. They stood in front of a dark gray stone building with ivy growing around it but there was nothing to suggest the size or location of the building. The older woman held something in her hand. Unfortunately, the image was too grainy for her to see clearly.

She tried being creative by, more or less, joining the dots but she still failed to identify it. Although, if she had to guess, she'd say it was a piece of organic matter, such as... a leaf, or a flower.

"Lady Woodridge, I have come to rescue you."

Hiding her surprise, Evie turned and smiled at Horacia Deblin. "Rescue me? From what?" And was that merely an excuse to once again engage her in conversation? Perhaps Horacia Deblin and Lady Moorsley had put their heads together to come up with a series of questions to...

Evie blinked. She had no idea where her mind was trying to lead her.

"I have made the rounds and heard the same stories told countless times last year," Horacia explained. "Do yourself a favor and seek solitude, as you are doing. Although, please, allow me to join you again. Even Gracelyn has succumbed to the spirit of the gathering and can talk of nothing but fishing."

"I'm not actually seeking solitude on purpose, I can assure you," Evie said. "When I visit a house, I am always intrigued by the personal touches on display." She set the photograph down. "I've been trying to place that image."

"Oh, that's Bramswood," Horacia said and added, "The academy."

Evie must have looked puzzled because Horacia went on to explain, "Gracelyn and I attended the same school for ladies, although at different times. That's Gracelyn in the photograph."

Pleased to have had one identity confirmed, Evie asked, "And who is the other lady?"

Horacia's chin lifted. Smiling, she declared, "That is Anita May Conway, the headmistress and shaper and nurturer of young minds."

"You say that with a great deal of admiration," Evie observed.

Horacia nodded. "It's easy to admire her. She is the type of woman we, at the academy, all aspired to eventually become."

"And have you succeeded?" Evie asked even as she

wondered how much of a person's life could be devoted to a single pursuit. In this instance, a pursuit of obvious excellence.

"I do believe I am well on my way. One can only aspire to greatness. Whether or not one succeeds in achieving it is an entirely different matter."

Curious, Evie asked, "How exactly did she shape your mind?"

Horacia leaned in and whispered, "By challenging me. Take, for instance, my interest in history."

Evie winced. "I meant to ask you about your writing but I didn't quite know how to phrase the question. Perhaps I should be asking how you were drawn to such a historical figure."

Horacia Deblin studied Evie.

A burst of laughter from a group sitting near the fireplace drew Evie's attention away but she remained aware of Horacia's gaze on her.

She imagined the young author wanted to determine her level of interest or understanding of the subject, something that could only be determined by asking questions since, surely, one couldn't really judge a book by its cover.

"I was guided toward it," Horacia finally said. "In a most direct way. You see, at Bramwood, Anita May encouraged us to always head in the opposite direction."

"That sounds rather interesting. How exactly did it work?"

"I have always been drawn to the outdoors and open spaces. Horses and hunting and so on. I lived in my riding breeches. I still do, up to a point. Once a country girl, always a country girl. Anita May wanted us to investigate all the areas we'd never shown an interest in. There were too many for me to count, so I sought refuge in the library as a way of escape. Little did I realize Anita's prompt had already worked on me. You see, if I'd wanted to hide, I should have taken my horse for a very long ride." Horacia's smile suggested she had been rather devious. "For some reason, I found myself needing and wanting a quiet spot to curl up in silence while everyone went on a frenzied search for the opposite of what they would normally do. I must have spent a week hiding out in the library, taking leisurely naps because no one else had thought to go to a dusty place filled with books. One day, I heard someone approaching so I picked up a book and pretended to read it." She nodded. "I became so engrossed, from that day onward, I worked my way through the vast collection. After reading many dozen books I realized they all had one thing in common. They'd all been written by men."

"And you are now intent on changing that?"

"I've become quite absorbed in the task." Horacia tilted her head and smiled at Evie. "I'm more interested to learn how you became involved in investigating crimes."

Heavens, not again… "By sheer accident."

Horacia nodded. "Anita May would love that."

The remark made Evie wonder if the subject had been discussed between Horacia and Lady Moorsley.

"I suppose I'm more interested in you as a person. Something about you must have drawn you in, like a magnet. Perhaps an inner desire to seek out the truth."

Oh, heavens, she was being called upon to explain herself. A part of her wanted to say she was Evangeline, the Countess of Woodridge and that entitled her to the right of never having to explain or apologize for her behavior.

To Evie's relief, Tom joined them and she was spared having to come up with an inspiring anecdote about her experiences as a lady detective.

"Please tell me you're not discussing ideal fishing spots," Tom said.

"Oh, good heavens, why would we do that?" As far as Evie knew, you claimed a spot, cast your line, and then played a game of patience.

"You'd be surprised." He glanced around him and lowered his voice. "There are high stakes involved. I suggest heading out early tomorrow. We wouldn't want to lose our place by the lodge."

"He's not wrong," Horacia said. "All this might look harmless on the surface, but everyone wants to catch the biggest fish."

"How odd. I never noticed." Evie glanced at the other guests and tried to see them in a new light. Cutthroat came to mind. She tried but the idea refused to take. Surely they meant to make a game of it all.

Horacia checked her watch. "That's the dressing gong."

Evie hadn't heard it. However, a second later, the clock on the mantle struck the hour followed by the resounding boom of the dressing gong.

Like the well-trained houseguests they were, they made their way out of the drawing room with the other guests following.

Crossing the hall, Evie saw Simmons, the butler, standing beside the bronze gong, almost as if he'd taken up his place to ensure everyone followed his strict protocols.

Deciding this would be a good time to steal away and compare notes with Tom, Evie nudged him and signaled toward the stairs. Knowing Tom, he would have found a way to dig up some information. Although, they hadn't quite decided what they were looking for, or even if they had any reason to be suspicious of anything or anyone.

Walking slightly ahead of them, Horacia turned, "I will see you shortly." She turned back toward the stairs as Simmons rushed across the hall toward the front door as if prompted by some unseen force about to descend on them.

Before he could reach the front door, it burst open and three young women waltzed in, laughing and chatting.

"Simmons!" one of the young women exclaimed. "Don't look so downcast. We've arrived in time to cheer you up."

Evie took a closer look at the young woman and immediately recognized her.

"Lady Constance." Simmons looked up at the heavens.

"Yes, I know... When will I ever grow up?"

Simmons turned to the other two young women and greeted them, "Miss Beatrice and Miss Ada. Welcome back to Allenford Castle. It's been..."

"Seven days," Ada grinned.

Simmons straightened. "Yes, indeed. Well, to some, seven days can seem like an eternity."

All three teased him by bobbing a curtsey and giggling like the school girls they were not.

Evie couldn't remember Constance's exact age, but she knew she'd already had her coming out presentation and ball.

Smiling from ear to ear, Constance rushed toward her. "Evie! You came. Mama said you would but I didn't quite believe her. It's been years."

Evie made the introductions and saw Lady Constance's eyes brighten with interest.

"Handsome," Lady Constance remarked as she studied Tom.

"Are all young women so forthright?" Evie asked.

"Yes, absolutely. We learned the hard way we might only have today and must, therefore, make the best of it." Lady Constance glanced at Tom and winked.

Evie couldn't help leaning in and whispering, "Please stop flirting with my fiancé." As she straightened, she saw one of her companions, Ada, looking quite pale. The cheerfulness of a moment before had completely disappeared and was now replaced by a look of stunned silence or shock. Evie couldn't tell which but it was definitely a negative reaction.

Ada's eyes were lowered but a moment before, she must have been looking at someone or something. Had she noticed someone she hadn't expected to see?

Simmons clapped his hands. "Lady Constance, the dressing gong has been rung. You must hurry along now. You don't want to be a stray kitten and make a late appearance."

Ada snapped out of whatever had taken hold of her and headed straight for the stairs.

If Constance had noticed her friend's behavior, she didn't say anything or give any indication she was in any way concerned by her friend.

Beatrice Hammond gave Constance a tug, and said in a tone dripping with honey, "Come along, Connie. You mustn't tease Simmons. Remember, he's our ally."

The butler gave them an indulgent smile and sent them on their way.

CHAPTER 6

When Evie and Tom reached the top of the stairs, Evie tugged him along a hallway, saying, "A private word with you, please."

Tom's eyebrows shot up. "What did I do?"

Surprised by his reaction, Evie narrowed her gaze. "Nothing. Why?"

"Your tone, it sounded as if you were about to scold me." Tom shook his head. "Never mind. What's worrying you, Countess?"

They reached the long gallery and walked along it, with Evie pointing to the river's edge that appeared from between a copse of trees.

"Yes, it's all very lovely but I know you didn't come here to discuss the view. What's worrying you? Has something caught your attention?"

She tugged him further along until she felt sure they wouldn't be overheard. First, she told him about noticing both Gracelyn and Horacia looking at her.

"Maybe they liked your tweed suit," he suggested. "Or... wait," he turned her around and tapped the back of her head. "Your hair was sticking up."

"What? Don't be silly. They were looking at me as if trying to determine something."

"Such as?"

"What does she know? Does she know something? Does she suspect us?"

"Us?"

"Does she suspect me... or you?"

"And you think they were both entertaining the same questions?"

Evie gave a reluctant nod. "They attended the same academy. Maybe they were taught to follow a certain train of thought." As Tom stared back at her, Evie began to realize how nonsensical she must have sounded. However, she knew intuition had a place in any investigation or pursuit of clarity, so she stood her ground.

"They might be puzzled because you made such a fuss about the flowers," Tom suggested.

"I made a fuss? What are you talking about? I merely asked about them. And, if you recall, Gracelyn found their presence quite odd too. I believe she means to get to the bottom of it."

"Really? I thought she'd dismissed it all."

"No, she didn't. She followed it up with her butler." Evie looked down the corridor. Lowering her voice, she said, "And just now, did you notice Ada? She looked as if she'd seen a ghost."

Tom looked around the gallery. "Do you know, that is something we haven't encountered. You would think that, somewhere in one of the many houses we've visited, we would come across a resident ghost, and that includes Halton House."

"You mean to say you haven't met Herbert?"

Tom crossed his arms and scowled at her. "You just made him up to satisfy my yearning to meet a ghost. It doesn't count. How are you going to produce him? Remember, I want to meet one and that means seeing it. I won't settle for a draft that can't be explained or the sound of chains rattling in the night. Or even a footman disguised as a ghost. I warn you, Countess, I will know if I'm being duped." He took hold of a strand of hair and teased her nose with it. Smiling, he asked, "What were you saying about Ada?"

"She reacted to something or someone she saw. I'm sure of it." Evie shrugged. "Well, at least I think she did. For all I know, she might have been lost in her own rambling thoughts and just remembered something that just happened to trigger her response of surprise."

Tom grinned. "I love it when you pose a question and then reason your way out of your suspicions."

"You're not being very helpful, Mr. Winchester." Evie tilted her head. "Then again… You have a way of challenging me that pushes me to seek further clarity." Evie gave a decisive nod. "We'll have to keep our eyes peeled open and observe Ada during dinner. If she falls silent, we might have reason to suspect someone's presence has rattled her nerves." Evie blinked several times, lifted her chin and rolled her eyes. "Then again, if she's chatty, she might be trying to disguise her concerns."

Tom grinned.

"Yes, I see your point. Now I'm thinking my remarks might suggest the presence of a shady area, something in-between." Evie sighed. "Well? Did you notice anything during your conversations with the men?"

"They were obsessed with fishing and nothing but fishing. Tomorrow promises to be an interesting day. More so, I believe, since I heard Horacia's remark. If the fishermen are more competitive than we previously thought, these next few days could prove to be quite interesting and revealing."

Evie puzzled over his remark. Had he tried to direct her thoughts away from her growing suspicions? If she could even call them that. So far, she had simply noticed a few oddities which could be dismissed as chance coincidences. After all, she insisted, those particular flowers were in season.

"Tom, have you been humoring me?" She didn't really need an answer. They often found themselves drawn into situations where they could sense something happening but couldn't proceed with any degree of confidence without first finding a significant connection or lead.

"Rest assured, I'm just as curious as you are."

Evie nodded. "But you're being sensible and stepping back to see what happens next." No point in forcing something that may or may not happen. Step back, observe and avoid setting off alarm bells by drawing attention to themselves.

He pushed out a breath and looked down for a moment.

"What?" Evie prompted.

"I'm not sure... Are we still curious about Enid Carlton?"

If she said yes, would Tom suggest returning to the village to discover what they could? Would simple curiosity be enough to draw them away from the fishing trip?

When she didn't answer straightaway, he said, "I take it we are merely observing and, dare I say it, absorbing?"

She gave him a brisk smile and surprised him by saying, "We are here to catch some fish."

"Very well. I'll go along with that."

"That's not to say we should let our guards down... Tom, do please try to be more observant during dinner. It would help to compare notes."

"Is that your way of saying I need to pull up my socks. It's suddenly become quite clear to me, you brought me here under false pretenses." When Evie didn't ask for an explanation, he added, "You tricked me into thinking this would be a fishing trip. Instead, we're fishing for who knows what."

"Oh, dear. You saw right through my ruse." Evie tapped her finger against her chin. "Did Simmons actually say he would try to find out where the flowers had come from?" Smiling at Tom, she sighed. "Fine, you're right."

"I didn't say anything."

"But you meant to."

He raked his fingers through his hair. "Remind me again what it was I was going to say?"

"Never mind. Come along, or we'll be late for dinner." She crossed her arms, uncrossed them and slipped her hands inside her pockets. Huffing out a breath, she clasped her hands…

"I can see you're really missing Holmes."

~

As she changed for dinner, Evie found herself thinking about secrets.

The many bouquets of flowers she had seen at the cemetery had all been the same but had, presumably, been sent by as many individuals.

They all shared something in common.

They all knew the deceased preferred those flowers.

Only one bouquet had been accompanied by a card and a message.

You will be missed.

Could she assume all the absent mourners knew each other?

"A secret society," Evie mused.

A secret sisterhood?

Tilting her head, she wondered why her thoughts had meandered along that path. She reached for her handbag and drew out her small notebook. Opening it to a clean page, she uncapped her fountain pen and made a note.

"Bramswood Academy." Looking up, she added, "I wonder… What if Enid Carlton had attended the academy… That would definitely tie a random encounter to other people." And that, Evie told herself, would be far-fetched.

Yet…

Quite possible. After all, they hadn't searched for the information. It had simply been handed to them when Horacia Deblin had told her about Bramswood Academy.

Had she just made a connection?

"To what?" Evie had to remind herself of the fact no crime had been committed. Also…

She had no way of proving Enid Carlton had attended the academy, certainly not right that minute. She supposed she could start by asking Gracelyn…

In the next breath, she asked herself, "How can we be sure no crime has been committed?"

Enid Carlton had been young. They should at least find out what she had died of. Tapping her finger against her chin, she thought about the solitary figure at a funeral service. Had Enid Carlton only recently met the maid or had she known her for a while?

What could the maid reveal about Enid?

"She could definitely tell us why no one else attended the service."

Sitting back in her chair, she drummed her fingers

and looked down at her notebook. Was she trying to look for a crime were none existed? Closing her eyes, she groaned. What on earth had possessed her?

She knew she should close the notebook and forget about it all. "Just put it all out of your mind and concentrate on catching the biggest fish in the river. That should put a few noses out of joint. Not that I really want to do that…"

Scooping in a breath, she opened her eyes and wrote Enid Carlton's name. "It's the flowers," she insisted. "They absolutely have to mean something."

The edge of her lip kicked up. "Only because they happened to catch my attention and, at some point, I might wish to concede the fact they are nothing more than a seasonal coincidence." Just… not right that minute, she thought and resumed thinking about secrets.

Enid Carlton had been young. Evie thought about her own youth. Those years had been carefree and her secrets quite innocent, but not everyone led such a humdrum existence.

What sort of secrets did she keep and had she taken them all to her grave? She'd been so lost in her thoughts, she didn't hear Rose come in.

"Milady?"

Evie emerged from her reverie and caught sight of her reflection in the mirror. Her eyes looked back at her as if from a distant land. The thoughts she had been entertaining scattered, leaving behind nothing but a trace of hints and suggestions.

Perhaps they were pursuing nothing but a fruitless endeavor. Even so, she preferred to err on the side of caution and keep her eyes open.

"I'm sorry, Rose. I was miles away." And muttering nonsense. Heavens, what had Rose made of it all?

Rose held up two headbands for Evie to choose from, once again catching her by surprise.

"Oh, dear…" Evie looked at one and then the other. "I'm sure either one will do. You decide."

"Me?"

"You're likely to make a better choice, Rose. I trust your instinct." Evie looked back at her reflection. Could she trust her own instinct or should she step back, relax and enjoy her stay here?

"I think the plain one with the feather, milady. Yes, I think it suits you. That's not to say the other one wouldn't look good as well. Would you like to try both?"

"That won't be at all necessary, Rose. The plain one looks perfect."

Secrets! That's what she'd been thinking about.

And… they already had a lead.

What if Ada Hodge had noticed the flowers and understood their full significance?

Evie blinked and focused on Rose who stood in front of her, looking as if she expected Evie to say something.

The young maid looked at the headband she held. "But I haven't put it on you yet. It seems such a shame not to try both."

"Rose?"

The young maid's cheeks colored. "I'm sorry. I don't usually go on like this. Maybe you shouldn't call me Rose."

Heavens! Evie searched her mind and tried to remember Rose's family name. She couldn't remember Millicent ever sounding so confused and she'd allowed her previous lady's maid far more liberties.

In situations such as this one, she always wondered what Lady so and so would do.

She couldn't bring herself to be firm or, heaven help her, express displeasure. So she took the road of least resistance and allowed Rose to try both headbands on.

"Rose, what can you tell me about Lady Constance's friend, Ada?"

"Miss Hodge?"

"Yes, I suppose that's her name."

"Not much, milady. They are as thick as thieves and the household always knows to be ready for some sort of prank from them. Lady Constance thrives on it."

"Have they always known each other?"

Rose removed the plain headband and held it up to compare with the other one.

It seemed there would be no swift end to the maid's hesitation. If she had to wager a guess, she'd say Rose had run into difficulties and was determined to do a good job and avoid any negative outcomes. Although, Evie couldn't really imagine Gracelyn being hard on her servants.

"Rose?" Evie prompted.

"Oh, yes. They attend the same academy, Bramswood."

Bramswood?

Of course, it made sense. Constance's mother had attended the academy.

Evie took the plain headband from Rose's hands and placed it on her head. "Is this how it's supposed to go?" She knew it sat askew and she hoped Rose would be distracted by fixing it into place.

Was it possible? Could Bramswood Academy be some sort of connection? Evie had no trouble imagining Tom asking about her imagined connection. He'd at least give her a lifted eyebrow look.

In a moment, she would be joining Tom and they would make their way down. How would he feel about traveling back to the little village and chatting with Enid Carlton's maid? She would bet anything they would discover a trail back to Bramswood Academy.

Would Tom try to talk her out of it? Would he want her to provide ten good reasons why they should abandon their planned first day of fishing to go chasing after a suspicion?

It wasn't even that. She would be more inclined to call it a curiosity, like an itch she needed to scratch.

"You were right, milady. This one suits you best."

"I believe you were responsible for selecting it, Rose. Thank you."

Evie swept out of the maid's reach to prevent any further fussing with her appearance. "Yes, I will be quite presentable, thanks to you."

As she hurried out of the room, she tried to remember what else she had intended asking the maid.

Pranks.

What sort of pranks did Lady Constance and her friends play?

She looked over her shoulder and shuddered at the thought of returning. Rose could take it as a sign she wasn't entirely pleased with her headband or her dress…

CHAPTER 7

*T*om stood waiting for Evie at the top of the stairs. When she reached him, he cupped her elbow to lead her down. Leaning in, he whispered, "They're up to something."

"They?"

"Lady Constance and her friends." He gestured to his tie. "I was struggling with this wretched thing and distracted myself by looking out the window. That's when I saw them sneaking out of the house."

Evie looked up at him, her eyes widening with interest. "How could you tell they were sneaking out?"

Lowering his voice, he said, "They hurried out and headed toward a copse of trees and disappeared into the forest."

"How odd. What could they possibly be up to?" Evie wondered if it might have something to do with the pranks they played. She shared Rose's remark with him and watched his reaction.

"I see." Tom frowned. "What sorts of pranks?"

Evie opened her mouth to speak only to realize she hadn't asked Rose for details.

A rush of heat surged to her cheeks. She didn't want to admit to hurrying out of the room because she'd wanted to escape the maid's incessant fussing.

"I hope they don't plan on scooping all the fish out of the river," Evie mused.

Tom leaned back and gave her a wide-eyed look of utter astonishment that the idea would even occur to her. "I've never heard you suggest anything so macabre and cruel."

Tom's response more or less answered her earlier question. He really was keen to spend a day fishing.

"Did you see all three rushing out?" Evie asked.

He nodded. "Although, one appeared to be lagging behind. Almost as if her heart hadn't really been into whatever they were getting up to."

"Could you tell which of the three lacked enthusiasm?"

"Despite noticing, I'm afraid I didn't pay much attention."

She would bet anything it had been Ada Hodge. Using her scolding tone, she said, "Tom, we're supposed to be observant and vigilant."

Tom grumbled, "I was struggling with my tie. In any case, is there a difference between one and the other?"

"What?"

"Being observant and vigilant."

"Oh… Probably not. I'm just making sure you

realize we're on the lookout for signs. Do try to focus. Your mind can stray to fish tomorrow."

"I can guarantee you fish will be on the menu tonight, and I don't mean on the plate in front of you."

They reached the bottom of the stairs and he signaled toward the drawing room. "Shall we?" Even as he asked, Tom's gaze drifted toward the flower arrangement behind them.

Evie looked heavenward. "Onward, Mr. Winchester. We are here to be sociable."

They found everyone in the drawing room enjoying very fashionable cocktails. Glasses glinted pink, red, green and even blue.

As they walked in, they heard a man with a high-pitched nasal tone declare, "Roving. There's simply no other way. Otherwise, you spend the day perched on a rock waiting for them to come to you. You must go in search of them."

"Clarkson, you know the fish are just waiting for you to walk away. They see you coming a mile up the river. I can just hear them, 'you know the drill. Not a bubble, not a ripple. This one always walks away'. Every year, you insist on employing the same tactic. Didn't get you anywhere last year. What are the chances you'll have a different outcome this year?"

Smiling, Tom and Evie wove their way around the room, and were not surprised to hear the same theme and similar secret tactics repeated in every conversation they overheard.

"You were not exaggerating. I honestly can't

remember everyone being so obsessed with fishing," Evie remarked. "At least you seem amused."

He grinned. "It's like being in a boys' club. Although…" he signaled toward a corner where two of the female guests stood chatting as they reeled in an imaginary line. "The enthusiasm has no barriers. Let's join them."

Sighing, Evie glanced over her shoulder and saw Lady Constance waltzing in by herself. Finding that strange, she searched for Ada Hodge and Beatrice Hammond. Ada walked through the doors but instead of joining Constance, she headed in the opposite direction and sat down in front of the fireplace.

Evie then spotted Beatrice. She stood with a group of men and appeared to have livened the conversation as they all laughed at something she said.

Aha, the *coquette*, life of the party and center of attention, Evie thought.

Did she pull the strings, influencing her friends, leading and misleading them?

Tom handed her a drink and raised his glass in a toast. "I got us a *Slippery Fish*." He winked at her. "We get to name our cocktails."

"Oh, what fun. What's in it?" She studied the glass and saw an elegant little curl of something she couldn't quite identify.

"Apple juice and vodka. The apple peel is supposed to be the slippery fish." Tom glanced away and murmured, "All three troublemakers are here."

"Yes, but they're not together." And whatever they

had been up to, hadn't taken long to achieve, she thought. Taking a sip of her drink, she smiled. "I have no idea what we're expecting to happen."

"A prank. I don't know about you, but I'm on guard and ready for anything. Do please watch my back."

"Your back? Do you think they'll target individuals?"

"I'd feel more comfortable if I could keep the dark-haired one with the sparkly eyes in my sights and at a relatively safe distance."

"Beatrice Hammond?" Evie whispered as she glanced her way.

Tom gave a small nod. "She looks shifty."

"Shifty?" Evie laughed. "If I didn't know better I'd say you feel threatened, Mr. Winchester."

"All I'm saying is that I'm going to watch out for that one."

"The gentlemen seem to be enjoying her company. Maybe you should warn them off her."

"It might be too late for them. She has them mesmerized. Look at her, all smiles, nudges, winks and laughter."

Evie smiled at his serious tone. Tom had, no doubt, stared down any number of dangerous situations. She couldn't believe he would really feel threatened by a delightful young woman. Then again, she had already labeled her a *coquette*.

Simmons, the butler, gave a discreet nod and, a moment later, Lady Moorsley invited everyone to proceed through to the dining room.

The lively discussions about fish continued even as everyone settled down in their places.

Constance and Ada sat on one side of the table with Beatrice sitting opposite them, all three forming a triangle which, Evie thought, would be interesting to observe.

How would they communicate, if they had to? Did they have predetermined signals to launch their pranks?

"I'm on edge," Evie admitted as she took her seat. Tom, as usual, ignored protocol and sat next to her.

"I'd like to say I'll keep you safe but who's going to keep me safe?" Tom murmured.

The twinkle in his eye suggested he had, indeed, been jesting. Then, Evie saw him straighten and turn slightly. When she saw him sitting upright and his shoulders stiffening, Evie leaned forward and noticed Beatrice had moved places and now sat next to Tom.

Straightening, Tom looked down at his cutlery and rearranged them.

Heavens, she could almost imagine him breaking into a sweat.

Leaning in, she whispered, "Tom? You're looking a little pained. Is something the matter?"

"Nothing at all," he said through gritted teeth.

Indeed. So why did he sound pained and discombobulated?

Glancing up, Evie saw Simmons following the progress of the footmen serving the first course. He lifted his chin slightly and Evie noticed he was now looking straight at Beatrice.

Leaning forward again, Evie saw the young woman turning toward the butler.

"Simmons, do please make sure the gramophone is brought down to the drawing room. We must have dancing. Yes, we must." Beatrice then turned to Tom and gave him a bright smile. "Please say you enjoy a dance, Mr. Winchester."

Tom swallowed. "On occasion." He twirled his knife and then tapped it lightly against the table.

"Fabulous. Then we must make sure tonight is an occasion. I just know you'll be light on your feet. Now Simmons, do please remember. We mustn't disappoint Mr. Winchester."

Simmons glanced heavenward. Evie studied him for any tale-tell signs of disapproval and found none. Indeed, when he composed himself and resumed overseeing the footmen, the edge of his lip kicked up, almost as if in amusement.

Evie turned to her dinner table companion on her right and smiled.

"Lady Woodridge. I'd heard you were back in England."

She studied the man's face and tried to see past the layers of time. His angular features looked familiar. In a moment of clarity, she remembered he had been a second son seeking his livelihood in a legal capacity. Of course, that had all changed when his older brother had perished during the Great War.

"Mr. Reed."

"Ah, yes. You do remember. However, do please call me Nelson."

Local gentry, Evie thought. The countryside abounded with gentlemen who somehow managed to get on without the added attributes of a title.

As Nelson proceeded to share his fishing secrets, Evie's attention drifted to Constance and her friend, Ada. They both sat opposite her and, without much effort, she could see their glances crossing over toward their co-conspirator, Beatrice Hammond.

"Is it true you have become involved in detective work?" Nelson asked and did not wait for an answer, "it sounds like an intriguing endeavor. I must admit I rather enjoy a good detective story. Do your cases resemble those of Sherlock Holmes?"

"I'm afraid our deductive work often resembles pure guesswork," Evie admitted. "With a great deal of creativity thrown in."

Nelson gestured toward Constance. "What would you guess Lady Constance is up to? I've noticed a few exchanged glances across the table and to her other young friend."

Surprised by his observation, Evie said, "There is a rumor suggesting they are up to something. Although, what that might be, I'm sure I couldn't say."

"They cut the lines last year."

"They?"

"All three. They sabotaged all the reels. It must have

taken them hours to unwind them, make the cut and then wind them up again."

"Heavens. What happened?"

"Oh, there was no way of proving it. The Brigadier was livid and threatened to cancel Lady Constance's coming out but then Lady Moorsley intervened by saying it was surely the only way they could dispose of her. Clearly not, as she remains single."

Evie looked at the protagonists in that little drama. The Brigadier was holding an animated conversation with the guests sitting at either side while casting glances at his daughter.

Oh, yes... He had his eye on her.

His wife, Gracelyn, who sat at the opposite end of the table, appeared to be indifferent to the threat of a prank in the making. However, Evie could tell that wasn't necessarily the case as Gracelyn maintained a maternal watchful eye without making it too obvious.

Just then, Constance's voice hitched and her mother's gaze hardened ever so slightly. The warning was noted and Constance responded with a slight roll of her eyes.

Shaking his head, Nelson Reed murmured, "I just hope they don't scare away all the fish tomorrow."

Evie agreed with a smile. As she turned to Tom, she found him leaning toward her, sitting on the edge of his chair and about to slide off.

"Countess," he whispered in a harsh tone, "she has me cornered."

CHAPTER 8

*E*vie watched as Tom brought a morsel of food to his mouth and nearly missed when his dinner table companion, Beatrice Hammond, leaned in and whispered something in his ear.

Tom's cheeks reddened and a thick vein pulsed on his temple.

My heavens, Evie exclaimed in silence as she wondered what the young woman could have said to put Tom so on edge.

Any minute now, she expected to see him wedge his finger between his tight collar and neck to relieve the tension.

In his place, Evie would have issued a harsh rebuke.

"You'll give yourself indigestion, Tom," she whispered.

"At this precise moment, I would give anything to see the earth open up and swallow me whole," he whispered back and, once again, edged away from his feisty dinner table companion.

As expected, conversation revolved around the one and only subject on everyone's minds—fishing. Past triumphs were reminisced and celebrated, details quibbled over and stories altered and enhanced.

Throughout the entire meal, Evie watched Tom come close to breaking into an undignified sweat.

The moment the meal ended and Lady Moorsley gave the signal to leave the gentlemen to their cigars and brandy, Evie surged to her feet, walked around Tom's chair and reached down to lace her arm through Beatrice Hammond's arm.

Evie spoke in a quiet, authoritative voice, "Come along, dear."

Beatrice puckered her lips into a pout. "Such a pity. I'm sure the gentlemen would prefer to continue enjoying our company. Don't you find the practice of abandoning them tiresome and antiquated?"

Evie decided she had been too kind in labeling the young woman a *coquette*. Reckless and irresponsible seemed to suit her. When words and deeds crossed lines, she was bound to land herself into the sort of trouble she would live to regret.

Offering her a smile, Evie tugged her along. "Not today, no."

Making her way out of the dining room, Evie and Beatrice were joined by Horacia Deblin who speared a lifted eyebrow look at Beatrice and warned, "Don't you dare meddle with the fish tomorrow. I have a solid wager in place and I aim to win."

Having issued her warning, Horacia walked on ahead.

Beatrice snorted. "Someone is in desperate need of a little fun."

"Is that what you learned at Bramswood?" Evie asked.

Beatrice grinned. "I see, you've become acquainted with our little sisterhood."

"Did you enjoy your time there?"

"I most certainly did. Anita May Connors is an exemplary model for any young woman aspiring to something other than normal expectations."

Evie tossed the words around her mind and tried to understand what Beatrice had meant. "What did you end up aspiring to?"

Beatrice shrugged. "I went in there expecting to bide my time until I was presented and could find a suitable husband. Now…" she shrugged, "I wish to find a partner who will compliment me."

High expectations indeed. "And which characteristics do you expect him to espouse?"

"He should be adventurous. There is no sense in me settling for someone who wishes to follow the hunt and all the seasons that precede and follow it when my spirit is soaring and yearning for excitement." She drew in a long breath and exhaled it on a sigh. "I wish to climb pyramids and paddle up the Amazon River.

Cross the Sahara Desert on a hot air balloon and climb the tallest peaks and, oh... so much more."

"You would give up the creature comforts of home for a life of adventure?"

"In a heartbeat. I could settle for comfort in my old age but first I wish to explore and live life outside of my known world."

"And have you found the right man to whisk you away?" It only took a swift calculation to know it would have to be a special man indeed since most men of good social standing, prominence and significant financial freedom were tied to home and hearth. Or, rather, to vast estates requiring some of their attention, if not most of it.

Beatrice drew in a breath and huffed it out. "I might have but I think he might need some convincing. At the moment, he doesn't really know what he wants."

"And you aim to guide him to your way of thinking and enlighten him?" Evie asked as they entered the drawing room.

"Sometimes, people need a dose of encouragement." Giving her an impish grin, Beatrice excused herself and went to join her friends.

Evie supposed it didn't matter what one aspired to since Anita May Connors could cast a light on even the most mundane desire and enhance it until it sparkled with splendor.

She almost wished she had attended Bramswood Academy. Although, she suspected she might have ended up following the same path she now found herself on.

Looking around the drawing room she saw three other guests she hadn't met yet. Gracelyn stood with them and appeared to be engaged in a serious conversation.

While curious to learn who they were, Evie headed in the opposite direction and settled on a settee by the fireplace. As she made herself comfortable, Horacia Deblin joined her again.

Looking toward Beatrice Hammond, Constance and Ada, Horacia drew her eyebrows down and scowled at the mischievous trio. "They're up to something, I can feel it in my bones."

"I doubt it will involve the fish," Evie said as she tried to lighten the moment. "Constance wouldn't dare incite her father's wrath again. He might disown her."

Horacia snorted. "I'm almost ashamed to be a part of the sisterhood."

That was the second time she had heard the term used in reference to the ladies who had attended the academy.

"Is that how you all think of yourselves? A sisterhood?"

Horacia nodded. "It's a pact."

Evie's eyebrows curved up. "Whether you like it or not?"

"You don't get to choose family," Horacia explained. "Anita May Connors insists we owe it to ourselves to offer each other support throughout life. As women, we must stick together. There's no getting away from the fact we live in a patriarchal society, that doesn't mean we have to play by their rules. Not entirely."

Signaling toward the guests she hadn't met, Evie asked, "Are they Bramswood pupils?"

"Oh, yes. Gracelyn went to school with their mothers. They're five years older than Constance and Gracelyn is hoping they'll be a positive influence. One of them, Eleanor Stevens, has just announced her engagement. It's a fabulous match for her."

"Compatible?" Evie asked and added the term used by Beatrice Hammond, "or complimentary?"

Tilting her head, Horacia gave it some thought. "Not at all. She's quite the creature of the night. I know for a fact she wishes to travel abroad and live in Paris, Berlin and Budapest. He's tied to his estate and quite obsessed with it. She merely matches his criteria."

"How exactly does she do that?"

"By hailing from a suitable family. I foresee a battle of wills and a rocky end. Or perhaps not. She might bend to his will and settle for the life of privilege he can provide." Horacia shrugged. "I feel it's a letdown but that's only my perspective of the situation. I suppose I expect everyone to aim high."

"You think she's settling?"

"I couldn't really say. She knows what she wants. Perhaps she's found a way to get it, even with the wrong man."

"I'm beginning to think there is a sense of purity in your ideal."

"Oh, yes, indeed. I'm referring to love, of course. Nothing but the deepest love and so on would compel me to enter the marital state."

"Are you quoting?"

"I believe I am and, I must admit, I'm a late convert to Jane Austen's Elizabeth Bennet."

Evie smiled. "Someone you found among the shelves in your sanctuary?"

"Yes."

Evie studied the young woman. Dressed in a black and earthy toned evening gown with bronze highlights, she stood with confidence and an air of self-awareness. Her slanted eye glance around the room suggested she knew where everyone was and she merely wished to see if they had noticed her.

She was certainly no wilting lily.

Horacia shrugged. "I shouldn't judge. This is all her choice. No one is forcing her into it." In the next breath, she added, "It's not what we're encouraged to aim for. Marriage, that is."

Evie couldn't help thinking about the lost generation—those who had perished and those who remained but had fewer choices. "It seems she might be making the best of a situation that could easily turn bad."

Horacia hummed under her breath. "I think she duped us all by appearing to be a free spirit, eager to explore and discover. Perhaps even live on the edge with aspirations to becoming a bohemian."

"What about the others? Who are they?" Evie asked.

"The one with the bright red lipstick is Charlotte

Bronswell. Elizabeth Cleghorn is standing to her right. Oh, I see another new arrival. Claire Thatchet. She has a beautiful singing voice but refuses to perform in public. She could go all the way and become a legend. There might still be hope for her."

"And do they all have aspirations to marry someone who will compliment them?"

Horacia watched them in silence. "To be honest, I couldn't really say. If anything, I have come to learn one can never really tell what is going through a person's mind. On the surface, they might be an open book and quite clear about their likes and dislikes, as well as their intentions. However, deep down..." Horacia shrugged and lowered her voice to a murmur, "They might be hatching out a plan and aiming for higher stakes." Horacia pushed out a breath. "I need a drink. That way, I can justify my thinking and the words spilling out of my mouth. Would you like me to bring you a drink?"

"Oh, no. Thank you. I'm sure I need to keep my wits about me tonight."

Evie watched her cross the room and wondered why Horacia Deblin bothered entertaining opinions about someone else's choices. It seemed such a waste of time and effort. Smiling, she conceded the point and acknowledged the fact she had just expressed her own opinion on the matter.

Far too soon, Tom appeared at the door to the drawing room, his manner observant as he sent his gaze skating around the room, no doubt, Evie thought, trying to place Beatrice Hammond so he could steer himself in the opposite direction.

She was actually surprised to see him standing alone. In her mind, she could picture him allowing all the other gentlemen to walk in ahead of him, thereby using them as a shield. Then again, she didn't believe he had a cowardly bone in his body. Merely a few cautious ones.

His gaze landed on her and he hurried across the drawing room, his expressive eyes showing relief.

"When did women become so unashamedly *risqué*?" Tom demanded in a hard whisper.

Instead of providing an answer that made sense, she asked, "What on earth did Beatrice Hammond say to you?"

"It doesn't bear repeating," he growled.

"She needs to be put in her place. Be firm but polite, Tom."

"Oh, I aim to be both. She's asking for trouble." He glanced over his shoulder before adding, "She recited a poem and one line stood out. Something about a field of white blooms, tuberoses and snowdrops to be precise."

Evie gasped. "In what context?"

"It really doesn't bear repeating."

Had they come full circle? Why would Beatrice mention those particular flowers?

"Drink?" Tom offered.

"Yes, please." Although, a moment before, she had turned down the same offer from Horacia saying she'd wanted to keep her mind clear. If Horacia had been intrigued by the remark, she did not express it. Evie merely assumed the author would bide her time, help herself to a drink and then settle down to question her.

Sweeping her gaze across the drawing room, she saw the wayward trio engaged in an animated conversation. They certainly looked excited about something. She watched Beatrice Hammond for a moment and did not see her attention stray from her friends. Not even when Tom walked past her.

Whatever they were discussing had her full attention.

Tom held out a drink and settled down beside her. "Here you are."

"Brandy?"

"Did you want something different. You didn't specify."

Taking a quick sip, Evie shook her head.

Tom glanced around. "Don't look now, Horacia is studying you."

Again?

"I was rather hoping she'd join me again. I wanted to ask…" Evie frowned.

"What? Don't leave me in suspense."

"Enid Carlton. Earlier, I had the craziest idea. Do you think it's possible…" she shook her head. "No, surely not."

Tom rolled his eyes. "I can't agree or disagree until you tell me."

Evie took a moment to allow the thought to settle

in her mind. "All the women here have one thing in common. They all attended the same academy." She pushed out a breath filled with frustration. "It's those flowers. Now more than ever I feel they tie everything... everyone together."

Tom glanced away briefly. "I believe Horacia has just interpreted your remark. She straightened and is looking directly at you. I find that rather curious."

"Tom! I can't tell if you're being serious or not."

"Oh, yes, indeed. I am being very serious." Tom gave a slow nod. "I'm beginning to think we have actually stumbled upon something of interest. Perhaps even intrigue." He took a sip of his drink and added, "Either that or our imagination has become highly active."

Evie drew in a long breath. "Fine, I'll tell you, but you must promise you won't laugh."

He held up a finger and drained his glass. "I'm ready."

"I think I might have entertained this idea before. Or, it might have been hovering in the back of my mind. I'm not sure... What if Enid Carlton attended Bramswood Academy?"

Tom responded by raising his glass to his lips again only to realize there was nothing left.

"Too far-fetched?" Evie asked.

He shook his head. "When we set off from Halton House, we were on a straight trajectory here."

"Are you suggesting we followed a trail and it led us to the right place, at the right time?"

CHAPTER 9

The next morning...

"*N*ine o'clock is too late, Countess. I guarantee all the good spots will be taken," Tom complained. "I don't see anyone else and I was the only one sitting down to breakfast. That means they all left at the crack of dawn."

Evie stifled a yawn. She had stayed up until the small hours of the night trying to make sense of the conversation they'd had the previous evening the only way she knew how, by writing a letter.

That morning, she had addressed the missive. Now she held the letter in her hand and could sense herself having second thoughts about it.

A problem shared, she hoped, would be a problem

halved. She and Tom were still waiting to take on their first assignment and were using the time to become acquainted with Lotte Mannering's *modus operandi* as each case she tackled had a different approach. From the start, Lotte had thought she and Tom would provide a different perspective and way of doing things. She had insisted their way of doing things would suit her just fine. It didn't matter how they got their results, just so long as they got them.

Evie hoped their current situation fit the bill.

With any luck, Lotte Mannering would be able to cast some light on her thought processes. Either that, or she would have a good laugh over her obsession.

As a lady detective, she needed her observation skills to be honed to perfection, as time spent chasing a false lead could cost her.

Burdening Lotte with nothing more than an inkling might not be the best way to impress the lady detective. The fact she was willing to risk making a bad impression suggested she was in dire needs of assurances.

When had she become so needy?

The previous evening, they had not been able to follow up on Tom's observation of Horacia Deblin's behavior because the author had made a discreet exit.

One moment she'd been there and, in a moment of distraction, they had missed seeing her leave the drawing room.

Had it been a deliberate attempt to avoid them?

If, as Tom had suggested, Horacia had been able to

read and interpret her expression, she might also have sensed Tom's remark about her watching them. Surely, she must know there would be no avoiding them forever...

Could Horacia Deblin be hiding something or did she merely consider herself the guardian of the sisterhood?

To Evie's relief, instead of dismissing her suspicions, Tom had said they'd set out from Halton House on a straight trajectory to Allenford Castle. Almost as if they'd been meant to come across the burial service.

Tom stood at the bottom of the stairs, his foot tapping an impatient beat. "Countess! Do hurry."

"Oh, Tom. There's plenty of fish for everyone." Reaching him, she adjusted her wide brimmed hat, tipping it back, only to look straight into his scowling eyes. She laughed. "And, suddenly, this has turned quite serious."

When she glanced across the hall and toward the dining room, Tom shook his head. "It's too late for breakfast."

"Tom, you don't seriously expect me to step outside without sustenance."

"Dieting is very fashionable." He rolled his eyes and shrugged. "Not that you need it."

"I should think not."

Digging inside his pocket, he drew out a little parcel. "I saved you a piece of toast."

Evie stifled a laugh. "Oh, how very kind of you."

He looked heavenward. "I'm sorry. I have no idea what's come over me."

"If you want my opinion, actually, you'll get it whether you want it or not... You are facing a dilemma."

"Me?"

"Yes, you. Tom Winchester, the man who always remains calm. Suddenly, you feel torn between wanting to do some fishing and, doing what is quite obviously the right thing to do."

"And what might that be?"

"Pursuing the trail of breadcrumbs we have set out for ourselves."

"Our imaginary trail." He pushed out a breath. "Yes, it is there, I'm sure of it."

Evie nodded. "You're probably struggling with it all because you are always the voice of reason. You stand back and take your time studying the situation. While I run around pointing fingers and coming up with the wildest ideas." Evie grinned. "I believe we make an excellent team." Giving a small nod, Evie turned toward the front door. "Since you are so eager to get started, shall we?"

He looked down at the little parcel containing his meager offering.

"Never mind that," Evie said. "You meant well and I'm sure I can wait until we catch our first fish. Perhaps you could light a little fire and cook it for me."

Tom pushed out a long breath. "I checked all the

newspapers. I just don't understand how something could have happened..."

It took a moment to remember the precautions Tom had taken before they'd set out on their trip, such had been his eagerness to spend a few days without distractions.

"There, there. Crime has no rhyme or reason and, do please take comfort, we haven't really discovered anything yet."

"You know what Henrietta would say to that."

Evie searched her mind. Henrietta had many opinions about many subjects but she didn't think she'd ever heard her discuss criminal activities. "What would she say?"

Tom rolled his eyes. "I have no idea but I do know she would have something to say. I almost wish she had come along."

A footman hurried toward them. "Lady Woodridge... Graham, the Brigadier's man is waiting for you outside and Cook has prepared a basket."

Smiling at the footman, she said, "That's very kind. Thank you."

Tom slipped the little parcel inside his pocket. "Just so you know, it's not just a piece of bread. I also added some kippers."

Evie snorted. "Tom, out of sheer curiosity, was that piece of bread really meant for me?"

Tom slipped his hands inside his pockets and murmured, "Well... When you didn't come down to breakfast, I assumed you were playing your lady of leisure card by having breakfast in your bedchamber."

"Have you ever known me to play that card?"

"No. But there is always a first time."

"I'll concede that point. However, knowing me as you seem to do, did you really imagine there would be a first time, especially since we are both clearly quite preoccupied with something that might or might not be a crime?"

Tom nibbled the edge of his lip. "Are you making conversation or do you really want me to answer?" He sighed. "Fine, the sandwich was for me but I had been willing to share it with you."

Evie hid her smile.

They walked out and were greeted by the splendid sunshine that was bound to make their early morning start pleasant.

Graham, the Brigadier's man, stood by a farm buggy, his arms folded across his chest, his attention fixed on the horizon. When he heard them, he turned and tipped his hat.

"You must be Graham," Evie said. "I hope we haven't kept you waiting."

He gave a barely perceptible shake of his head.

"I take it the others have already sought out their prime positions." Evie thought she heard Tom grumble under his breath.

"Aye, they're all set up. Not to worry, you're headed to the lodge. It's one of the best spots. There's a little bend and the fish linger for a while before moving on."

Tom helped her up onto the carriage and pointed to the basket. "Look, there's food."

Evie smiled at him. "You could say you had a lucky escape."

Tom grinned. "Or, I could claim responsibility for the basket."

"Remind me never to come between you and your fishing." Evie set her handbag down and, as she looked up, she met Tom's frown.

"You didn't," he said.

"Didn't what?"

Lowering his voice, he whispered, "Bring the revolver."

"I might have."

He nodded. "Perhaps it's just as well."

The Brigadier's man got them on their way and, within a few short minutes, they had crossed a bridge and were winding their way along the opposite side of the river.

"I don't see anyone. Do you? They must be well-hidden."

"Tom?"

"Mmm?"

"I honestly can't tell if you're being serious or not and it's beginning to worry me."

"Yes, I can see your point." He reached for her hand and took it in his. "It's that damn little flirt. I have this constant urge to look over my shoulder."

"She really has you rattled." Had Beatrice Hammond

been lewd? Evie couldn't think of any other reason for Tom to feel as he did.

She knew good manners would compel him to remain civil. That meant she might need to step in and deliver a few harsh words.

Changing the subject, Evie said, "I wrote Lotte a letter last night. I felt the need to clear my head and introduce some order in my thinking."

"Did it help?"

She supposed it had. "I'm sure I know what her response will be." Evie tipped her head back and sighed. "No crime has been committed."

"And yet... we can't ignore everything we've noticed. You should listen to your instincts. They have served you well in the past."

Evie glanced up at him. "Do you realize what that means?"

He held her gaze for a moment. "I'm sure it means our fishing trip is about to be cut short. Then again, the village where Enid Carlton is buried isn't very far from here. I think we could dash down, ask a few questions and be back in time to hear all the tales of triumph from today's fishing. Although... I can't see why we couldn't enjoy today and do our snooping around tomorrow."

Evie groaned. "If only we had thought to do all that before setting off here." Belatedly, she wished they had lingered and asked questions right then and there.

"Yes, if only. However, at the time, we were only

dealing with a curious encounter. Now... Well, now we have tuberoses and snowdrops to join the dots."

They fell silent.

Evie found the prospect of trekking back to the village daunting. She couldn't even begin to imagine what they might find there.

Worse.

She might discover her observations and growing suspicions were groundless and that could shatter her confidence.

She knew they would head straight for Enid Carlton's house and, with any luck, they might be able to speak with the maid they'd seen at the funeral. It had only been a day and she was probably in the process of closing the house. What guarantee did they have the woman would even speak with them and reveal personal information about Enid Carlton?

"Here we are." Graham brought the buggy to a stop, hopped off and unloaded the basket. "All the fishing rods and bait you'll ever need are inside the lodge."

Helping Evie down, Tom looked up at the building. "This is a lodge? I was expecting some sort of rustic log cabin. This is a mansion."

The stone building had columns flanking the wide entrance and the mullioned windows echoed the design of the castle. "I can't see the damage from the storm but I'm not complaining."

The Brigadier's man set up a small table and a couple of chairs near the water's edge. A perfect choice, Evie thoughts, as the sun had chased away the morning's chill turning the little beach area into an ideal spot for breakfast.

Thanking him, Evie said, "We'll take it from here. Thank you, Graham."

As she settled down to her first cup of revitalizing coffee, Tom went inside the lodge and, soon after, emerged with a selection of rods.

A moment later, he stood beside Evie, his attention on the water.

"I brought you one too. It's fairly light." Glancing down at her, his eyes filled with amusement. "Did that sound patronizing?"

"It could have been worse. You might have said it's light enough for me to look quite fashionable. Would you like some coffee?"

"No, thank you." Tom stepped forward and, without further preamble, he cast his line. A moment later, the line tensed.

Surprised, Evie asked, "Oh, did you catch one already?"

He stood still for a moment and then eased back down onto his chair. "False alarm."

Evie sipped her coffee at leisure and took in the calm surroundings. If they could have a couple of hours of peace and quiet, she could call this little venture a success.

Her mind emptied for a fraction of a second before she asked, "Do you think last night's prank was actually planned for today?"

"I've been scanning the area and haven't seen any

sign of anyone being near us," Tom murmured. "I can't imagine what they would get up to."

"That's just it. I'm sure the mischievous little trio can be quite creative and will surprise us all with their antics."

They both fell silent. Evie's thoughts strayed to the previous evening and to Horacia Deblin's behavior. It had seemed odd. Far too obviously so. What could have prompted her to distance herself from them?

She knew there could be any number of reasons for Horacia Deblin to have left the drawing room early.

She might have had an inspired idea and had retired to her room to work on it. Or she might have wanted to get an early night. Or, despite her keen interest to learn all she could about private detectives, she might even have found the company dull.

Evie set her cup down on the table and stood up. Picking up her rod, she walked a couple of paces toward the shore and gazed across the water.

Gentle ripples formed a pretty pattern on the surface. She couldn't tell if they were made by insects or by fish. Maybe both, she thought and hooked her bait.

Testing the weight of her rod, she cast her line. If anyone was watching them, they would think they were both keen anglers, intent on catching the biggest fish.

Tom sat back, the picture of perfect relaxation. She had no way of telling if his mind was on the fish or everything they had talked about.

Turning slightly, Evie asked, "Did you share any of your tactics with the guests last night?"

Tom shrugged. "I would have if I had any."

Evie snorted. "And here I was, thinking you were about to impress me."

"Watch and learn, Countess." He picked up another rod, hooked his bait, cast his line, lowered his cap over his eyes and sat back.

"Aren't you worried the current will carry your line or tangle them?"

Tom shook his head. "Either the fish find the bait and take the hook or they don't."

Evie frowned. Was he trying to confuse her?

Instead of watching his rod, his gaze wandered around their little beach. "Still no sight or sound of the others," he mused. "They can't be far."

Evie resumed watching her line and considered the possibility Tom had been in a hurry to get here so he could be present when something happened. He was clearly expecting something to happen. "It's a long stretch of water, Tom. There is plenty of room for everyone."

"And plenty of trees to hide them. They could be watching us as we speak."

"Why would they do that?"

"To employ the element of surprise, of course."

"To what end?"

His eyebrows shot up and he growled, "I have no idea and that is driving me to distraction."

Evie laughed. "Perhaps that is their prank. They

want everyone to think they are plotting something and then... they sit back and watch everyone on tenterhooks."

Tom narrowed his eyes and shot to his feet.

Startled, Evie asked, "What is it?"

He gestured to the right. "Do you see that?"

"What?"

"There's something floating down the river."

CHAPTER 10

"What is it?" Evie asked as she narrowed her eyes. "Oh, oh… Is that what I think it is?"

Tom nodded. "A garland. I'm going to guess and say they're tuberoses and snowdrops. Although, to quote you, good heavens, what are the chances?"

Evie gaped at the flowers.

As they watched the garland float by, they noticed more garlands following in its wake.

"This must be the prank they'd planned." Shaking her head, Evie added, "I fail to see the point. Do you think there's some sort of hidden meaning?"

Tom shrugged. "Some sort of funereal send off for all the fish? That's my guess."

"It looks harmless enough," Evie said. Although, she wondered what the fish would make of it all.

They both leaned forward and looked toward a rocky outcrop and the bend.

"There are more coming," Tom said.

The procession of garlands floating by kept them captivated until, suddenly, a flock of birds took flight.

"There's someone out there," Tom whispered.

They heard a mixture of running footsteps and gasps. Someone was running through the brush but they couldn't tell from which direction the steps were coming from or even heading.

Evie was about to say sound traveled over water and caused distortions when they heard a yelp, followed by a scream.

Tom and Evie stepped forward, the tips of their shoes right at the water's edge.

"That sounds like more than one person running," Evie said. In the next breath, she added, "Was that a splash?"

The next yelp they heard, this time louder, seemed to suggest someone had fallen into the water.

"That definitely sounded like a splash." Tom took a tentative step and another. "I think it came from..." he growled. "No, I can't tell."

The lodge was located in a natural cove with bends on the river on either side. If Tom wanted to follow the sound of the splash, he would have to climb over a rocky outcrop.

"What the devil," someone yelled. "What are you doing there, you silly girl. Get out of the water."

The Brigadier.

Tom appeared to get his bearings. Following the sound of the Brigadier's outburst, he rushed toward the bend on the right, with Evie following several paces behind.

"Constance, get out of there at once," the Brigadier hollered. "You're scaring off the fish."

"It's not Constance," someone yelled back. "It's Ada. Ada Hodge."

"Quit flapping your arms. You'll only make it worse."

As they rushed toward the sound of voices, they ran out of shoreline and had to maneuver their way along the rocks.

Finally, they made enough headway to see Ada in the river, her arms flapping about as she struggled to keep her head above water.

"Stay here, Countess." Tom made quick work of removing his coat and shoes. He rushed in, running along the shallow water as far as he could and then plunged in.

As she watched, Evie tried to figure out how Ada had fallen into the river. She must have been on the other side of the shore where the water was deeper. A path followed the water's edge on higher ground. She couldn't tell for sure, but it looked as if the path might be quite narrow.

But why had she been running?

Evie could only guess she and the others had been responsible for the garlands floating along the river and had been trying to escape the scene of their crime.

Or...

Maybe someone had been chasing her.

She scanned the length of the opposite shoreline for signs of someone watching as well as the others. Constance and Beatrice had to be nearby.

If someone had been chasing Ada, had they meant to cause her harm? And, if so, why?

Finally, Tom reached the young woman, wrapped his arm around her waist and pulled her toward the shallow end.

Despite his larger frame, it took some doing to get Ada to calm down and help rather than hinder their progress.

Ada coughed and sputtered but, otherwise, seemed to be fine. When they were at waist level, Tom propped her up beside him and coaxed her along.

Reaching the shore, Tom set her down and stepped back to catch his breath.

Evie rushed forward but had no idea what she could do other than to offer assurances. "You're safe now."

Ada gasped in a breath and pressed her hands to her chest. "Oh, my goodness."

"Ada, what happened?" Evie asked.

The young woman raised a hand to her face and moaned. "That was… quite intense and frightening. It caught me completely by surprise."

Evie heard the Brigadier approaching and muttering under his breath, his determined steps sending a few loose rocks rolling down to the water.

When he reached them, he glared down at Ada. "What the devil were you doing in the water?"

"I… I must have slipped."

Evie's eyebrows curved up. That had been her first thought and it would only make sense if Ada had been rushing or distracted by something or someone.

The Brigadier looked at Tom. "Just as well you were here and took prompt action. Thank you." Swinging around to face Ada again, he demanded, "Where are the other two? I swear I'm going to put that girl over my knee. I warned her to stay out of trouble and now look at what she's done."

It seemed Constance would get the blame no matter what. Evie lifted a hand to shield her eyes from the sun and searched the bank. Still no sign of anyone else. If, as she suspected, someone had been chasing Ada, they were either long gone or doing a very good job of staying out of sight.

"It was an accident," Ada murmured.

"Nonsense," the Brigadier said. "There's no such thing as accidents. Only carelessness." He looked up and around him again. "Someone's gone to fetch Graham. He'll be along soon. There, there, don't cry."

"I'm not crying," Ada wailed.

The Brigadier bent over her. "Is anything broken? Do you feel any pain?"

"No. I'm just wet."

"The sun will dry you in no time. Graham will take you back to the castle. You'll be your old self again in no time. Lady Moorsley will make sure of that."

For some reason, the Brigadier rolled his eyes.

Evie exchanged a look of confusion with Tom. She

wanted to have a private word with him but decided to wait until they were alone again.

Turning back to Ada, Evie asked the obvious question which Ada seemed intent on ignoring, "How did you fall in?"

"I... I must have slipped. It just happened," Ada insisted.

The Brigadier straightened and looked toward the river. "Well, that's that then. You've scared off the fish. I'm going to round everyone up and we'll all head back to the castle. Yes, I think that's for the best. There's no use grumbling over uncooperative fish and young women falling into the river." He stepped away only to stop and turn back. Wagging a finger at Ada, he said, "Let this be a lesson. You know it could have turned out very badly. Yes, indeed. You had a lucky escape."

Half an hour later, Graham, the Brigadier's man appeared.

Helping Ada onto the buggy, Tom and Evie climbed in and they all made their way back to the castle.

Along the way, Evie tried to coax Ada into explaining how she could have lost her footing.

"What were you doing?"

Ada shook her head. "I must have been distracted. I think I saw a pretty bird and then... I heard a noise in the bushes. It all happened too quickly. I don't know... The Brigadier was right. I was careless and wasn't watching where I was going. I should have known better."

Evie looked away and into the distance. After a

moment of clearing her mind, she looked back at Ada. "What happened to your fishing rod?"

Ada looked away. "I... I must have dropped it in the river."

Tom scowled at her. "Were you responsible for the flowers floating in the river?"

Ada's cheeks colored but she didn't answer straight-away. "Flowers?" she eventually asked. "What flowers?"

"There were flowers floating in the river," Tom said. "Specifically, garlands of flowers. Someone went to a great deal of trouble."

"I... I didn't see them. Oh... wait a minute. Maybe that's what distracted me. Yes, that would have been a curious sight to see." Ada shrugged. "I'm not sure if I thanked you, Mr. Winchester. I was ever so lucky you were nearby to rescue me. I'm not the strongest swimmer."

Tom gave her a small nod and sat back. "Yes, you were lucky but something tells me circumstances put you in that spot at that precise moment."

Ada stared at him and blinked hard as if trying to follow his reasoning.

"Oh, never mind all that." Crossing his arms over his chest, he looked away.

Sitting next to him, Evie could see his jaw muscles hard at work. She imagined he was only now thinking about the dangerous situation he had been plunged into.

Ada could have suffered a worst fate.

~

When they arrived at the castle, two footmen rushed out and tried to assist Ada inside but she insisted she was perfectly fine and only needed a hot bath and a change of clothes.

Tom and Evie stood at the foot of the staircase. When Ada reached the top landing, Tom asked, "Well? What do you make of all that?"

"I don't know. It all sounds rather odd. I find it difficult to believe she just slipped." Something happened and Evie suspected no amount of prodding would compel Ada to talk about it. "Also... this is not something new."

"What do you mean?"

Evie sighed. "There was that moment, when Ada first arrived."

"Oh, when she looked as if she'd seen something or someone."

"Yes."

"Did we actually jump to conclusions? Do we think Ada saw the flower arrangement and reacted to it because..."

"Indeed, because... Well... because..." Evie pushed out a hard breath. "We don't know what meaning the flowers hold and yet we are convinced they do hold some significance."

"I agree." Tom hitched his wet coat over his shoulder. "I should go change into something dry."

There was no question of returning to the lodge.

Evie went up to her room and changed her clothes. Just as she finished adjusting her blouse, Rose walked in.

"Milady!" Rose pressed her hand to her throat. "Oh… oh, dear. I'm ever so sorry. You gave me a fright. I didn't expect to find you here. And… Oh, dear… I shouldn't be saying all this."

Evie rolled her eyes. She knew servants were trained to be invisible—not seen or heard. However, as Millicent had pointed out, she was rather unique and unconventional and didn't abide by rules.

"That's perfectly fine, Rose. I'm not surprised I frightened you. Mr. Winchester and I had a rather bad experience and I am probably showing it."

"Is this about Ada Hodge falling into the river?"

"Oh, I see word has already spread."

Rose nodded. "Her ladyship is beside herself with worry. She feels she's responsible for the young ladies here and worries she might, one day, need to deliver bad news. They're all in the drawing room talking about it."

Evie considered going down and joining the group. "I thought the other guests had all gone fishing." The Brigadier had said he would round everyone up but Evie hadn't believed they would all be willing to give up their day's fishing.

Rose nodded. "They just returned. As soon as word spread about Ada falling in, they all decided to abandon their efforts and try again tomorrow. They're funny that way. They seem to think it's put a jinx on the fishing."

Evie looked at the clock on the mantle.

"I believe refreshments are being served, milady."

As she tidied her hair, Evie tried to picture Lady Moorsley being beside herself with worry. It seemed like an uncharacteristic reaction.

Yes, she would express concern and take measures but then she would compose herself and continue on with her day.

Rose looked down at a skirt she held folded over her arm. "I came in to return this skirt. Earlier, I saw the hem was coming loose so I thought I would… fix it. I mean… I hope you don't mind."

"Rose." Evie smiled. "If anything, I'm the one who shouldn't be here right now." Everyone knew bedchambers were to be made available to the servants for cleaning and tidying during the day. Returning to it at any time other than for dressing and sleeping only threw everything out of order.

Giving herself a final once over, Evie walked to the door. "I'll get out of your way now." She hurried out and down the stairs, this time not bothering to wait for Tom. She trusted he would eventually find his way down to the drawing room.

Halfway down the stairs, she heard several voices then she saw the guests who had been out fishing making their way in.

They sounded jovial enough. When she reached the bottom of the stairs, however, she took a closer look and saw quite a few scowls and frowns.

Yes, most of the guest were making the best of the

situation by embellishing stories about the fish that got away but it was clear they were not at all happy to have their fishing disrupted.

Evie searched for anyone not showing any signs of being cross.

Someone in the group had to be responsible for chasing Ada Hodge.

CHAPTER 11

It came as no surprise to see the first guests to head to the drawing room were the women while the men lingered in the hall. As practical as ever, Evie thought. With the day's fishing ruined, the women took a moment to rest and enjoy a cup of tea.

Evie followed them in and found Lady Moorsley sitting with Eleanor Stevens and two other women Evie didn't recognize. She assumed they had only just arrived. They were about the same age as Eleanor Stevens so Evie guessed they had also attended Bramswood Academy.

Horacia Deblin sat near a window, her attention on the cup she held. If she had any interest in the conversation taking place, she did not show it.

Noting her entrance, Gracelyn, Lady Moorsley, beckoned Evie over. "Come sit down and tell us what you saw. We've only heard a brief version of events. Graham is never forthcoming with much information.

Certainly not more than is absolutely necessary. He simply does not care to embellish. And the Brigadier is not making much sense. I daresay, we already have next year's topic of conversation. Indeed, we will all be talking about this for years to come."

"There really isn't much to say. Ada Hodge fell in the river." Evie made sure she glanced at everyone's reactions.

The two newcomers looked surprised.

Eleanor Stevens remained expressionless. Then, she lifted an eyebrow and said, "Careless."

Evie nodded. "That's what the Brigadier said."

"It goes to show they were only there for a lark," Eleanor Stevens said.

"I can't believe Constance. She's been warned. I hope she knows more," Gracelyn said. "The little devil is hiding somewhere. Out of sight, out of mind, she probably thinks but she couldn't be more wrong. The Brigadier will have a few words to say to her and he's probably rehearsing them as we speak."

"I can tell you Tom fished Ada Hodge out of the river. She kept herself afloat but I'm not sure how long she would have lasted." Evie helped herself to a cup of tea and lingered near the table. Or, rather, near Horacia Deblin. She had positioned herself as an observer rather than a participant.

"That was very gallant of Tom," Gracelyn said. "Eleanor says there were flowers in the river."

Evie glanced at the bride to be who nodded and

said, "I saw a garland drift by. Shortly after, I heard a yelp."

"What an odd thing to see," Gracelyn exclaimed. "What do you suppose it means? We get all sorts of things drifting in the river but I've never heard of a garland."

"Tuberoses and snowdrops," Evie mused.

"What?"

Nodding, she took a sip of her tea. "I didn't see it up close but that's what it looked like. Just like the display in the hall."

Gracelyn shuddered, "I still don't know where those came from."

As Evie took another sip of her tea, she glanced at Eleanor Stevens and realized she must have been close to the Brigadier.

A few of the male guests drifted in and headed toward the table to help themselves to some refreshments. They each had their own version of events and where quite precise about where they were when they saw the garlands drift by. It seemed they had been launched from several places.

Sidling up to Horacia Deblin, Evie smiled at her. "Did you see or hear anything?"

Horacia straightened in her chair. "I'm afraid I missed all the excitement. I was furthest from the lodge than anyone else. Since Tom Winchester rushed to the girl's rescue, I assume that's where all the action took place."

"What about the garlands? Did you see them?"

"No." Horacia shook her head. "The fish weren't biting so I decided to walk back. I'm not surprised by that now, what with all the commotion."

"Out of curiosity, what was your tactic?" She must have had one, having gone so far as to place a wager.

Smiling, Horacia shrugged. "I placed myself furthest away from everyone thinking the biggest, strongest and most cunning fish would elude everyone and eventually make its way up to me. It wasn't exactly the most inspired strategy but I had some thinking to do. So I didn't mind biding my time."

"Ideas for your book?"

Horacia studied Evie for a moment. It seemed to be a habit with her. Either that, or she was deciding how best to answer.

"Just thinking. It's an exercise I employ to broaden my thoughts. I never have a particular subject in mind. Somehow, thoughts crop up in my mind and I spend some time entertaining them, keeping the ones I find interesting and discarding the rest."

Evie was about to ask if Anita May Connors was responsible for teaching her that particular trick when another thought strayed into her mind. "I wonder if you might know…"

Horacia tilted her head. Instead of encouraging her to ask, she studied her in the manner that was clearly her trait.

Hesitating, Evie searched for the right words. "How acquainted are you with the students who have attended the academy."

"I take it you are referring to past students rather than present student."

Evie nodded.

"I'm sure I'd be able to recognize many names but I doubt I can claim to know everyone."

That seemed to be a fair assessment. Deciding she had nothing to lose, Evie said, "Enid Carlton."

Horacia's eyes wavered for a moment, moving from left to right as if searching for an answer. "For some reason, I feel the name should sound familiar." She gave it some thought and then shook her head. "I can't place it. Would you like me to ask around?"

"Yes, please."

Leaning forward, Horacia's eyes widened slightly. "May I ask why you want to know? Is this part of an investigation?"

Evie didn't want to share her suspicions. Certainly not until she felt she stood on firm ground and had something solid to go on with.

"I came across the name and thought I heard it linked to the academy." As soon as she spoke, she wished to take it all back. She didn't want to mislead anyone with her wild assumptions.

Also...

Horacia Deblin had been the first to mention the academy.

Would she make the connection?

Exasperated with herself, she looked away and saw Tom standing at the door.

He glanced around the drawing room. When he saw her, he nodded and beckoned her over.

"Would you excuse me, please? I've been summoned." Relieved to escape the awkward situation, Evie hurried her step. When she reached Tom, she smiled. "I knew you'd find your way down."

"Did I just rescue you from something?" he asked.

"You most certainly did. I'm afraid I blundered."

"You? I find that hard to believe." Tom guided her out of the drawing room. "What did you do?"

"Before I could think better of it, I mentioned Enid Carlton's name."

"Why on earth did you do that?"

She gave him a pointed look. "I didn't think there'd be any harm in it. Now, I'm not so sure. There is something odd going on here. Add to that our curiosity about Enid Carlton and I believe I might have put us at a disadvantage. Now someone else knows we know Enid Carlton."

"And that would be bad because…"

Evie shrugged. "If, hypothetically, we did actually stumble upon something, Horacia Deblin now knows we might be aware of it. She might mention it to someone else and… Well, word might spread and…" Evie glanced over her shoulder. "Someone in there might have something to do with…" Evie stopped and lifted and dropped her shoulders.

Tom smiled. "That's right, we don't know. Might I suggest we simply proceed with an assumption."

"I'll take whatever suggestion you are about to offer."

"Let's simply assume we are on the right track and our supreme observation skills have led us to uncover some sort of nefarious activity, which we will eventually expose."

Evie studied him for a moment. "Did you just come up with all that?"

Tom grinned. "Your reasoning skills are rubbing off on me. Now, to tell you what I have discovered."

"Oh, you actually have something new to add." She leaned forward and adjusted his tie. "That's better. So… what did you learn?"

"When I made my way down, I met with one of the other guests and stopped for a chat."

"Did he give you a name?"

"Nelson Reed."

"Oh, he's lovely. What did he have to say?"

"He had a spot near the Brigadier and he thinks he saw the garland when it first appeared on the opposite side of the river."

"What do you mean?"

"He said he saw it appear on the edge of the bank. We saw it floating along the middle of the river."

Evie's lips parted. "Oh, I've just thought of something." She went to stand next to Tom and turned so she had her back to the front door and the river beyond. "We were both looking this way." She pointed straight ahead. Then she moved her finger to the right. "You spotted the garland coming from our right."

Tom nodded.

Evie pointed further to her right. "The Brigadier was just over the bend and you say Nelson Reed had a spot near him."

"That's correct."

"Oh, I've lost my train of thought."

Tom rolled his eyes. "Do you need a prompt?"

Evie moved her finger. "Wait a minute, I think it's come back. If Nelson Reed saw the garland on the opposite side of the river, then the person who put it there…"

As Evie's voice trailed away, Tom picked up the thread and continued, "Was on the other side of the river."

Swinging around, Evie faced the front door. "It's higher ground so they would have had the advantage of knowing where everyone was."

They both fell silent for a moment.

Then, Tom spoke up, "We know Ada Hodge was on the other side of the river and we assume the others, Constance and Beatrice, were with her."

Evie glanced at him. "And we suspect they weren't alone." Her finger jutted out and she swung toward the drawing room. "Someone in there was also on the other side of the river and they are responsible for launching the garland."

"Garlands. There were quite a few of them."

All along, they had suspected Constance, Beatrice and a reluctant Ada. What if the garlands had been launched by someone else?

Evie shared her thought.

Tom looked heavenward. "In that case, we'll have to obsess about the meaning of those damn flowers."

That wasn't all they would have to obsess about, Evie thought. The person responsible for launching those flowers, was quite possibly also responsible for bringing them into the castle and putting them on display in a prominent area where everyone arriving would see them.

Were they meant to convey a message? And was the message supposed to be understood by a select few?

The sisterhood.

Now more than ever, Evie believed the flowers they saw at the cemetery held a deeper meaning.

Could they reveal something about the absent mourners?

"There's something else." Tom reached for something in his pocket.

A newspaper.

"When I went up to change clothes, I came across something." He unfolded the newspaper and showed her an article. "It's yesterday's newspaper."

"Good heavens," Evie exclaimed as she skimmed through it. She read the article again with greater care. "Anastasia Gregson a former pupil of Bramswood Academy."

Tom nodded. "The funeral was attended by family."

With substantial flower offerings of tuberoses and snowdrops.

She searched for the date and gasped. "The funeral

was held three days ago."

Tom surprised her by saying, "It's just on eleven. If we set off now, we'll arrive at the village before midday."

"The village where Enid Carlton lived?"

He nodded.

Evie read the notice again.

Tom raked his fingers through his hair. "Do you remember all those newspapers I organized to be sent to us at Halton House?"

She nodded.

"I searched through every single one of them looking for any odd occurrences of criminal activities."

"And you found none."

He nodded. "When I saw this notice, it triggered something. I don't know why I didn't think of it before. I mean, at least when you brought those flowers to my attention the first time we saw them at Enid Carlton's funeral."

"Are you about to tell me you remember seeing other notices?"

"At least one other."

Without saying another word, they both rushed upstairs to collect their traveling coats.

~

Evie took a moment to scribble a note. She read through the brief outline, folded the piece of paper and slipped it inside an envelope. Addressing it to Millicent at Halton House, she slipped it inside her pocket and was about to rush out of the room when the door opened.

Rose stepped inside and yelped. "Oh, dear. I did it again."

"Rose, just the person I wanted to see." Evie retrieved the envelope and handed it to the maid. "Would you make sure this is posted as soon as possible, please."

"You're entrusting me with a letter. It sounds rather urgent."

"It is. Are you able to get away?"

"Oh, yes, of course."

"Also..." She picked up her handbag and looked inside to make sure she had everything she needed. "If anyone asks, Mr. Winchester and I have driven off and, while we will do our best to return in time for dinner, we might not actually make it back. In which case, no one should worry about us."

"This sounds intriguing," Rose said. "Although, I'm sure it's not my place to ask, so I shouldn't... I mean, I won't."

Nodding, Evie walked to the door only to stop when Rose called out, "Your hat, milady."

"Oh, yes... of course. Thank you." She turned back and, to her dismay, saw two hats on the bed.

"Which one would you like, milady?"

Knowing what was to come, she reached for both hats. "I'll take them both, Rose. Just in case one blows away."

CHAPTER 12

Two hats are better than one

"Why do you have two hats?" Tom asked.

"It's rather a long story, Tom. Actually, I'd rather not say."

Tom held the motor car door open for her and smiled. "Now I'm curious. I'm afraid you'll have to tell me."

"Oh, very well. I'll tell you, but you must promise not to laugh."

Tom grinned. "But that's half the fun."

By the time they reached the gate to the estate, she had told him about Rose barging in and had managed to paint a picture of herself as too tolerant and perhaps even gullible.

"It sounds to me like you feel sorry for Rose," Tom said.

"Not at all. She just seems reluctant to commit to a decision. I'm sure if I hadn't taken the initiative, I'd still be there trying on hats."

Making the turn into the road, he glanced at her. "Are you about to make way for yet another lady's maid at Halton House?"

"Why would I do that?"

"Because you seem to think Rose is not entirely happy here."

He made a valid point. Being preoccupied with the business of the flowers and the funeral service they'd come across, she hadn't engaged Rose in conversation. Ordinarily, Evie liked to express some sort of interest, not just out of politeness. She was actually genuinely interested to learn where people where from and what they hoped to do in the future.

"Do you think she might need rescuing? I can't imagine Gracelyn being cruel to her." Evie gasped.

"What?"

"What if it's me... What if I'm the one making her nervous?"

"I sense you will want to compensate her for it."

"That goes without saying. When visiting other houses, it's actually customary to leave generous tips. I'm sure it's not something you need to concern yourself with since you never accept the assistance of a valet."

"I've been dressing myself all my life. Although...

there seem to be more and more distractions and now I find myself struggling with my ties. Perhaps it might be time for me to seek assistance."

"Yes, I can see what you mean about the distractions. Now I'm thinking about Rose. Asking if she's actually happy working here might throw her into a state of panic. I'm not sure I wish to risk it. Anyhow, even if she is unhappy and I offer her a place at Halton House, there's no guarantee she'll like it there."

Tom nodded in agreement. "She will either thrive at Halton House or run away screaming in fright at some of the things that go on there…"

There were three deaths that they knew of and they all had one thing in common. The same flowers. The very flowers which had also appeared at Allenford Castle, not once but twice.

Tom couldn't remember if the other notice had mentioned anything about Bramswood Academy. However, the flowers had definitely been mentioned. In any case, they now knew about two people connected to Bramswood Academy having died within a short time of each other.

"Cause of death," she murmured.

They knew Enid Carlton had died of natural causes. Could they trust that information?

Sometimes, what appeared to be natural causes could be a disguise for suspicious circumstances.

It only took a curious mind to raise the alarm.

She thought about Detective Inspector O'Neill. What would he say if she contacted him with the information? Would he follow through on it and look into the matter or dismiss her suspicions as inspired but lacking in substantial proof?

As much as the detective had come to appreciate their instinct for criminal activities, Evie doubted he would give them the time of day.

They needed solid proof of wrongdoing.

~

Sometime later...

"Did you know, during the Victorian and Edwardian eras, murder-sightseeing used to be a popular pastime? When a murder was committed, word would spread, and people would line up to have a look at the scene. I find the idea quite ghoulish. The fact it has gone out of fashion can only be ascribed to the wider variety of entertainment now available, I'm sure of it."

"You're saying people prefer to go to the moving pictures or to the seaside rather than to a murder scene?"

"Precisely."

"And yet, here we are," Tom said. "On our way to a

village to find out all we can about a woman we suspect met with foul play."

"Indeed."

The village they had stopped at the previous day came into view.

Tom slowed down. "Are we sure about this, Countess?"

"Absolutely. We have come this far, we might as well go all the way. We have nothing to lose and everything to gain if we happen to find something odd."

"You mean, something that fits our criteria?"

Evie nodded. "Yes."

Pointing ahead to the pub, Tom said, "I'll have to stop there and ask for directions to the house. We don't want to go knocking on the wrong door. That would only trigger everyone's curiosity."

Evie didn't want to say anything but she suspected their mere presence would raise a few eyebrows. Someone was bound to remember the motor car. They might even remember seeing them walking up to the church and stopping by the gravesite.

She searched her mind for the maid's name.

Alice Breer.

If they could establish a few facts, they might be able to dismiss their suspicions and return to the castle to spend a few days fishing and relaxing.

Although...

There was still the question of Ada Hodge's reaction when she'd first arrived as well as her plunge into the river.

Tom brought the motor car to a stop outside the pub. "I won't be long."

As Evie waited for him, she watched the comings and goings of life in a small village.

Despite it being midday, a time when everyone returned home to prepare meals, there were quite a few people out and about, carrying on their day's business.

A woman hurried along, a young child in tow. Judging by the way the little girl dragged her feet, they were headed somewhere she did not wish to go.

The woman carried a small basket, which she adjusted in her arm. Looking down at the little girl, she spoke to her, her facial features soft and devoid of any sternness. Evie felt glad for the little girl and gave the woman credit for appearing to employ a calm approach. At least the little girl wasn't being scolded and made to feel worse.

When the woman stopped and bent down to rearrange the little girl's hat and coat, Evie decided they were definitely about to pay someone a visit. She imagined the woman saying they wouldn't be too long and it wouldn't hurt to be polite and smile.

The little girl pouted and nodded.

Whatever the woman said to her seemed to do the trick. Finally, she produced a smile and gave a vigorous nod.

The woman straightened and they continued on their way, the little girl now skipping beside her.

Evie continued watching them until they disappeared around a corner. Glancing away, she saw Tom approaching, his eyes lowered to the ground. That worried Evie. Had the maid closed up the house and moved away? It had only been a day.

Tom climbed in and sat back.

"Oh, Tom. You're keeping me in suspense."

He turned to her. "What? No, I'm not. I'm focused on remembering what the publican said about Alice Breer."

Evie gave him her full attention.

"She worked for Elizabeth Carlton since a young age. I suppose that's what you call a family retainer."

"Elizabeth Carlton? I take it that's Enid's relative?"

"Yes, her aunt. Anyhow, now Alice Breer is holed up at the house and refusing to see anyone. Apparently, she took Enid Carlton's death quite badly."

Evie straightened. That didn't bode well. They had driven all this way to get answers to questions she hadn't even given much thought to. Now they risked returning empty-handed.

"Did he provide the correct address?" she asked.

Tom nodded. "We're looking for the house with the tuberoses and snowdrops."

Evie tipped her head back and groaned.

"Chin up, we haven't failed yet."

Tom started the motor and wove his way around the village. When he stopped, he looked toward a lane. "The house is at the end." He growled softly. "I can see those tuberoses and snowdrops from here."

Seeing one of the front windows open and the lace

curtain billowing in the light breeze, Evie brightened. Alice Breer might not be receiving people, however, she hadn't entirely closed herself off from the world.

"Let's walk down," Tom suggested.

Evie felt her heart rise up to her throat. She knew they were about to impose on a woman who was clearly in mourning and she still had no idea how to broach the subject of Enid Carlton's death.

Grabbing hold of Tom's wrist, she gaped at him.

"What?"

"I'm… I'm all choked up."

"That's understandable."

She needed to grow a thicker skin. How else could she hope to barge in on people and ask pertinent questions?

"Take a deep breath," Tom suggested.

"I'm breathing."

"No, you're not. You're gasping for breath."

Yes, he was right. Nodding, she scooped in a breath. "Not a word to Lotte Mannering about this."

"Of course. We wouldn't want her to know you're human."

Evie gave his sleeve a tug. "Come along."

"I'm right beside you, ready to step in if you flounder."

"That's very comforting. Thank you." As they drew closer to the house, Evie realized she was probably most concerned about not finding answers. Although, it might help to know what sort of questions she should ask.

"I wrote Millicent a letter explaining what we were doing and I asked her to look through all the newspapers you received. I specifically asked her to pay close attention to any mention of the flowers."

"That's a very good idea. I might have missed something or someone else."

Evie shuddered. They already had two deaths to look into, with a possible third death, all connected to the academy and... the flowers. "I also asked her to make inquiries about Bramswood Academy."

"Don't you trust Horacia Deblin to provide you with the necessary information?"

"I think you know the answer to that."

"Do I? Please refresh my memory."

"Well, she is a graduate of a school. They refer to themselves as the sisterhood. Can we really trust her to be honest and reveal all she knows? Or is she likely to close ranks and keep secrets?"

Tom nodded. "What about Ada Hodge?"

"You saw how she reacted to my questions. She definitely knows something and she is being targeted. At least, that's my assumption."

Her step faltered. "Oh, heavens... Of course." She sensed Tom looking at her and before he could ask, she said, "Cause of death. We should start with that." Finally, she had a question she needed an answer to. However, she still needed to think of a way to approach the subject with Alice Breer.

"And how exactly will you explain our interest?"

"I've changed my mind. We should start by asking if Enid Carlton attended Bramswood Academy."

Tom nodded. "I agree. If the answer is in the affirmative, that should, at least, give us the proverbial foot in the door."

Suspicions and suppositions. That's all they had. However, Evie had to remind herself her hunches had often served her well.

Tom pushed open the iron gate and they walked up the path toward the front door.

Evie watched for any signs of movement or sounds coming from the open window. If, as Tom had said, Alice Breer hadn't been receiving visitors, it seemed unlikely that she would come to the door willingly.

The idea of making a pest of herself did not sit well with her but Evie felt she had to be ready to do whatever it took to speak with Alice Breer.

Rather than delegating the task, Evie stepped forward and knocked on the front door.

The little garden received the best possible light and it showed—its display of full blooms looking quite resplendent.

Everything looked neat and tidy, a sign someone took great care to perform regular maintenance.

She was about to knock again when the door opened a fraction.

Despite only catching a brief glimpse of her when they'd returned to collect their luggage from the pub, Evie immediately recognized the woman peering out at them.

Alice Breer's eyes narrowed slightly but not out of displeasure at being summoned to the door. To Evie, it seemed to be a reaction to the bright light of day. This suggested she had not ventured out that day.

She studied Evie and, after a brief moment, appeared to recognize her. "Yes?"

Evie apologized for the intrusion and introduced herself and Tom. "I understand this might not be the best time."

Alice Breer gave a small nod and, to Evie's relief, opened the door a fraction and asked, "What can I do for you, my lady?"

Evie offered condolences for her loss.

"I noticed you at the service. Did you know Enid?" Alice Breer asked.

"No, we didn't."

That seemed to puzzle her.

Evie considered handing her one of her lady detective business cards but then thought better of it. There was no point in alarming Alice Breer.

"We understand her passing came as a surprise."

Alice nodded. "It was sudden." She clutched her cardigan until her knuckles showed white. "One day she was perfectly fine and the next day she wasn't."

"So she didn't have a condition?"

Alice frowned. "No, she didn't. At least, not one that I knew about."

"Was the doctor able to identify a cause of death?"

"She died in her sleep. Natural causes... and..."

Alice Breer gasped and murmured something Evie didn't quite hear.

"I'm sorry, I didn't catch that."

"I wasn't here for her. I should have been, but I wasn't."

She appeared to be about to close the door. Evie wouldn't blame her if she did but she still needed answers.

"This might sound irrelevant. Can you tell us if Enid Carlton attended Bramswood Academy?"

Alice Breer straightened and her expression tightened. Once again, she spoke in a murmur, almost as if expressing a thought she hadn't really meant to share.

This time, however, Evie managed to decipher it. "So much for the sisterhood?"

"She always spoke highly of the school. I expected at least one representative to attend the service, but no one came."

"Perhaps news didn't reach everyone," Evie suggested.

Alice Breer shook her head. "I made sure to contact the academy." She frowned and looked over her shoulder. "Oh... I'm sorry, I just remembered I left the kettle on the stove." She gave the door a nudge to close it when she seemed to change her mind. "Would you... would you care to come in?"

CHAPTER 13

*A*lice Breer showed Evie and Tom through to a tidy drawing room furnished with some lovely pieces.

As Alice excused herself, Evie breathed a sigh of relief. This gave them the opportunity to delve deeper and she knew they had to.

While she wished to be wrong about Enid Carlton's death being suspicious, her intuition kept pointing at it.

A moment later, Alice returned carrying a tray which she set down on a piecrust table.

Evie decided to proceed by expressing an interest in Enid Carlton. "We understand Enid Carlton had only recently moved to the village."

Alice nodded. "She inherited this house from her maiden aunt and had been quite happy to settle here. She preferred a quiet life."

Just as Alice Breer picked up the teapot, Evie leaned

forward and, lowering her voice, said, "This might sound insensitive, but was there any question of looking into the death further?"

"What do you mean?"

"I'm referring to an autopsy to find out the real cause of death. I assume there wasn't one."

Alice hesitated. Shaking her head, she poured the tea. "I don't see why that would be necessary. The doctor knows his business and it's not my place to question him."

Not her place?

That struck Evie as an old-fashioned way of thinking. Then again, she had the advantage of a different upbringing, having been taught from an early age to question even those in positions of authority.

"Dr. Mason is a trusted village physician and an upstanding member of our little community," Alice added and shook her head. "No, it really isn't my place. It wouldn't be right. Besides..." She frowned. "I fail to say why her death would be suspicious. There were no signs of a break-in. Crime is not something we worry about in these parts."

Yet crime, Evie thought, did not discriminate.

"Do you know if she had been in touch with anyone from Bramswood Academy? Perhaps someone came to visit her."

Alice shook her head. "I'm sure, in time, she would have reached out. However, Enid had been dealing with her aunt's death. She'd also been too busy organizing the move here and wrapping up her life in town."

"Is that where she lived before?"

Alice nodded. "She had a position as a private tutor and had already applied for the role as school teacher here. Her aunt had already taken a turn for the worst and Enid had wanted to be with her. She came to stay with us as soon as she could manage it."

Evie looked about the tidy drawing room. Everything in its place and a place for everything. There were books and mementos on display. A flower arrangement looked fresh enough to suggest Alice had been mindful of keeping busy.

"Is there anything that might have looked odd to you? Anything at all?"

Alice was about to shake her head when she turned away and appeared to think about something.

Evie held her breath for a moment, then asked, "Have you remembered something?"

"I'm not sure." Alice handed Evie and Tom a cup of tea and sat back. Then, almost as an afterthought, she leaned forward and picked up her own cup.

Taking a pensive sip, she said, "Enid sent me away to town on an errand. She had forgotten a couple of things and had wanted me to fetch them. She insisted I stay on for a couple of days to visit my cousin. When I returned…" Alice looked around as if searching for something. Setting the cup of tea down, she stood up and walked to a bookcase. "I found this box on the table. It contains letters and photographs she sent her aunt throughout the years. The photographs were scattered on the table, almost as if she'd riffled through the box looking for something." She sat down and removed the lid from the box.

Evie frowned. "I'm sorry, this might sound insensitive, but… when did Enid die?"

Alice took a deep swallow. "While I was away."

Noticing her lip quivering, Evie leaned forward and took her hand. "You came back from town and learned of her death?"

Alice nodded. "That very morning. The next-door neighbor had come knocking at the door. She'd noticed the milk sitting outside. When Enid didn't answer the door, she let herself in. Margaret, that's the neighbor, called out Enid's name. When she didn't get an answer, she searched through the house and that's when she found Enid… in her bed, still dressed in her nightgown." Alice continued on in a flat tone. "I arrived later that day. Dr. Mason had already signed the death certificate."

So there hadn't been an autopsy.

How could that be?

If Enid Carlton hadn't had a history of ill health, surely there would have been some curiosity about the cause of death.

"How old is Dr. Mason?"

"Oh, he is getting on in years, although you wouldn't know it by the way he gets around, still tending to everyone's health, no matter the time of day or night. He has been the village physician for as long as I remember and I was born in this village. In fact, he helped bring me into the world."

Evie tried to estimate Alice's age. Late fifties?

Exchanging a look with Tom, Evie knew they were both thinking along the same lines. The good doctor's age might be reason enough to bring this matter to the attention of the authorities.

Looking down at the box, Evie asked, "May I see the photographs?"

Nodding, Alice handed her a stack of photographs. "They are mostly of her academy friends."

Evie searched for any familiar faces but found none. "If you don't mind me asking, how old was she?"

"Twenty-seven."

That put her in the same age range as some of the guests at Allenford Castle. She remembered Horacia saying they were five years older than Constance and Evie knew Constance was twenty-one, nearly twenty-two.

Alice sifted through more photographs and then handed them to Evie. They revealed just what she'd been looking for. Two familiar faces. She searched her mind for their names.

Charlotte Bromswell and Elizabeth Cleghorn.

Claire Thatchet appeared in the next photograph she looked at. The young woman stood next to Enid and they were both laughing.

Alice handed over more photographs. In the last stack, Evie found an image of Enid and Eleanor Stevens, the recently engaged graduate of Bramswood

Academy. They were both standing in front a door with ivy growing over it. She was sure this was the same door where Gracelyn had posed with Anita May Connors.

"Oh, that's odd," Alice murmured.

Evie looked up.

"There appears to be a photograph missing. I wanted to show it to you because it's one of the few images where Enid is with someone other than a friend from the academy. I've looked through these images so many times, I feel I know them by heart. Enid used to enjoy telling tales of her adventures at the academy. She loved sharing her recollections of her time there."

"Perhaps you missed it."

"Oh, no. I'm sure I've been thorough. Her aunt and I had entertained high hopes for her. Of course, we were both overjoyed at the prospect of Enid coming to live here but, in reality, we would have been over the moon with happiness if she'd settled down to married life." Alice shrugged. "Enid had been a romantic, always quoting Elizabeth Bennet from Pride and Prejudice. Anyhow, we thought this young man might be the one for her. She certainly held him in high regard and spoke of him often." She shook her head. "No, it's not here. Perhaps it fell when I gathered them and put them away. I shall have to search for it. Enid looked so happy in that photograph."

Tom broke his silence by asking, "Was there a hint of things getting serious between them?"

"Oh, I believe he is now spoken for. Whenever I

asked her about him, she'd say he still needed time to ripen. I never really knew what she meant by that. I could understand if she'd said he needed to sow his wild oats."

Tom nodded. "Maybe she meant to suggest he was still finding himself."

Alice set the box aside and sighed. "It's really rather odd. She was a romantic but she was never nostalgic. I can't imagine why she would have gone through this box without me being here to listen to her stories."

"Perhaps one of the neighbors dropped in for a visit while you were away," Evie suggested.

"It would have been a surprise visit." Alice shook her head. "Otherwise, Enid would have mentioned it beforehand. We'd actually talked about it. I usually have some sort of cake for afternoon tea but, what with one thing and another, I had been remiss. Enid told me she could live without cake for a couple of days and not to worry about it. Enid loved my Dundee cake and would have made sure I baked some to offer her guest."

It sounded like Enid Carlton had been eager to get Alice out of the way...

Was it possible there had been a mystery guest?

Someone not from the village?

Evie didn't wish to alarm Alice or trigger her suspicions without good reason. The poor woman had clearly been through enough.

"May I ask what is going to happen to the house now?"

Alice clasped her hands and pressed them against

her lap. "I should consider myself lucky. At my age, I wouldn't want to start looking for another position. Enid's cousin will be moving in soon. She's a spinster and is quite happy to move to a small village. I believe she has hopes of setting up a library here. She is a trained librarian and works in town."

A cousin? "Did she attend the service?"

Alice shook her head. "Diana had been traveling abroad at the time and couldn't get here in time."

It seemed strange that no one had been able to make the time to attend the service. "I hope you don't mind me asking, when you contacted Bramswood Academy to let them know of Enid's passing, whom did you speak with?"

Alice glanced away and then nodded. "The school secretary. She said she would make sure to inform everyone."

They had sent flowers but had not attended. These were, presumably, some of the people who appeared in the photographs.

Tom leaned forward. "Do the flowers... the tuberoses and snowdrops, hold any special meaning?"

Alice stared at Tom for a moment before saying, "They're the academy flowers." She searched through some of the photographs until she found the one she wanted. "See here, just above the door, the images are carved into the stone."

The door with the ivy growing around it.

Evie considered her next question with care. She knew she had to ask it. "This might sound odd... Do you know of anyone who might have wished Enid harm?"

Alice was quick to answer. "Everyone loved Enid. She never voiced a harsh word against anyone."

Evie thought she might have done so in private.

"Do you think the neighbor, Margaret, might have noticed someone coming to visit?"

Alice sighed. "She might have. However... Margaret's been busy with her daughter and her new baby. If she'd seen someone, I'm sure she would have mentioned it." Alice Breer pressed her hands together. "I'm beginning to wonder about all your questions. Exactly what is your interest?"

Evie did her best to explain. When she mentioned the flowers, she made a point of saying she had noticed only one card among the wreaths.

"I must say, I hadn't noticed."

But she had noticed the fact not one of Enid's friends had attended the funeral.

CHAPTER 14

After thanking Alice Breer for her time, they went next door and spoke with the neighbor. However, as Alice had explained, Margaret had been busy looking after her daughter and new baby.

They didn't need further convincing as the wailing they heard almost drowned out the conversation.

As they walked back to the motor car, Tom said, "Are we now considering the possibility of someone being responsible for Enid's death?"

"I believe we are open to all possibilities. It's called keeping an open mind and, considering what we've seen..."

Tom nodded. "Say no more."

Natural causes. Evie didn't understand how everyone had simply accepted that as the cause of death.

"I suppose that means you do not accept the doctor's verdict."

"The elderly doctor," Evie clarified. "He might have missed something."

Tom held the car door open for her. "I'm not being critical."

"I didn't say you were." She needed his voice of reason. It helped to consider all possible aspects.

Tom nodded. "This could well be the perfect crime."

"Precisely," Evie exclaimed. She climbed in and straightened her skirt. "Alice contacted the academy. She informed them about Enid's death. Some of her friends are currently enjoying a cup of tea at Allenford Castle." Evie stopped and considered what she'd just said. "My heavens. Either they know something about this or…" Evie shook her head. "At this point, I can't even engage my imagination." Could everyone be complicit?

Tom rounded the motor car and settled behind the driver's wheel. "Do you wish to speak with the doctor?"

"We should. Although, I suspect he will be quite dismissive of our interest. We don't really have any right to make inquiries. As for mere curiosity, well… anyone can be curious but that's not to say the good doctor needs to pander to us. I'm sure he's a busy man."

"That will be his problem to deal with." Tom started the motor and got them on their way. When he reached the main road, he stopped. "Of course, it might help to know where I'm going."

Evie managed a smile although she was far from feeling amused.

~

They returned to the pub and asked for directions to the doctor's surgery.

"I'm not sure if I should focus on the outcome I wish to have or expect the worst," Evie mused.

"Chances are the doctor will be set in his ways and not give us the time of day."

"I see, you are preparing for the worst." Evie lifted her chin. "Even if he did not detect anything suspicious about Enid's death, I find it difficult to understand why he did not wonder why a woman in apparent good health and with youth on her side would suddenly die." Evie huffed out a breath. "We might be doing the village a good service."

"By exposing his negligence?" Tom asked. "I hope this doesn't end with us being chased out of the village."

Tom found a place to park the motor and they walked the rest of the way.

"It's difficult to picture a murder taking place in this idyllic village," Tom remarked.

"It is lovely and, for that very reason, it would be the ideal place to set a murder. No one would suspect a thing."

"Was that meant as a harsh rebuke."

One filled with frustration, Evie thought. "You'd think someone might have noticed something amiss. And, now that I think about it, I assume Elizabeth Carlton lived here all her life. Why didn't the locals attend her niece's funeral service, if anything, out of respect for her?" From what Alice Breer had told them, Enid Carlton had been a regular visitor. She had not been a complete stranger.

Tom pointed ahead to a stone building next to the post office. "Here we are. Now, please remember to smile."

Evie glanced up at Tom. "Will you smile?"

"I believe my role is to look very serious."

They entered the surgery and approached a desk where a middle-aged woman sat at her typewriter changing the ribbon.

"I'll be with you in a moment." When she finished, she wiped her hands clean and smiled at them. "Now, how can I help you?"

Evie gave her a warm smile. "We would like to speak with Dr. Mason, please."

"Dr. Mason is making his rounds, visiting patients. Is this an emergency?"

"No, we only wish to speak with him. Do you expect him anytime soon?"

"I'm afraid I couldn't really say when he will return. Sometimes, he hurries along, other times, he lingers…"

Were they prepared to wait?

"Oh, look. You're in luck. Here comes Dr. Mason now. He looks rather pleased with himself but I'm not surprised. He's carrying a loaf of bread. It's his reward for dealing with young Jimmy."

Evie turned to watch his approach. The doctor did indeed look pleased with himself. Either he'd had a good outcome with the patient or he was simply pleased with his loaf of bread.

The secretary welcomed him with a bright smile. "Did young Jimmy give you any trouble?"

"Not at all. I told him if he bit me again, I would do some biting of my own."

The secretary followed the doctor into his surgery. A moment later, she emerged and said Dr. Mason would see them.

"Take care, Countess," Tom warned, "the good doctor bites."

"I have been warned," Evie murmured. Dismissing all her concerns, she gave the doctor a brief explanation for their visit.

Dr. Mason studied Evie for a moment and then moved on to Tom. Satisfied with what he saw, he said, "I see. And how did you know Enid Carlton?"

"We didn't. I suppose you could say we are merely expressing an interest."

"Out of curiosity?"

"Lady Woodridge is in partnership with a lady detective," Tom explained, "and she consults with Scotland Yard."

"That is very interesting," the doctor remarked. "And you say you are curious about the cause of death."

Evie nodded.

Dr. Mason brushed his fingertips along his chin. "I must admit, I did find it strange that someone so young should pass away in their sleep, but I saw no signs of...

what would you call it? Tampering? I assume that is what you're looking for."

"How closely did you look?" Evie drew in a deep breath. If she wanted the good doctor's cooperation, she might want to avoid questioning his abilities.

Dr. Mason sat back in his chair and swung from side to side. Stopping, he leaned forward. "I performed an examination."

"But not an autopsy."

Again, he sat back and brushed his fingertips along his chin. "How exactly did her death come to your attention?"

Although reluctant to mention the flowers, Evie couldn't think of anything else to say.

"What a curious observation."

"Lady Woodridge has a keen eye and the ability to connect the oddest things to criminal activity."

"Yes, I see, but… tuberoses and snowdrops? That's interesting. Did you know they are both poisonous?"

No, she hadn't known that.

"Here's another interesting fact about those flowers, in particular, snowdrops. You'll have to excuse my bluntness. The fact is, they have been used to induce certain outcomes in… unwanted pregnancies."

As he spoke, he watched Evie with great attention. Almost as if he wanted to catch her reaction. Indeed, almost as if he wished to make her uncomfortable or, rather, test her sensitivities.

He gave a firm nod. "There were no signs of

poisoning. Would you like me to provide a list of the symptoms and signs of poisoning?"

Evie declined the offer. She and Tom had already spent many hours researching the information. The usual symptoms included abdominal pain, lack of coordination, seizures as well as bodily excretions. The latter would have provided a clear indication of something worth looking into.

"Asphyxiation," Evie suggested.

He tapped his fingertips against his chin.

"If she had been asphyxiated by force, there would have been signs of bruising around her mouth and nose. I did not detect any. As it is, asphyxiation can occur in deaths from other, dare I say it, natural causes."

Was it possible she had simply died?

~

"You're not convinced," Tom said as they walked back to the motor car.

"It seems my silence speaks volumes."

Tom looked up and down the main street.

Sighing, Evie said, "We should return to Allenford Castle."

"I thought you were about to suggest we contact Detective Inspector O'Neil."

Evie studied him for a moment. When she spoke, she surprised herself by saying, "There is something we haven't talked about and now I'm thinking we should have. Motive."

"Why would someone want to kill two and possibly three women?" Tom asked. "To silence them."

To silence them because they knew something. Killers always had something to gain. Something that could be measured. Financial gain, came to mind. Unfair advantages. However, she knew some killers commit their hideous crimes for the pure pleasure of it.

When she shared her thoughts with Tom, he agreed. "It would be interesting if graduates of the academy were being targeted."

That would put all the female guests at the castle in peril.

He looked over her shoulder and nodded. "I believe we are being summoned."

Evie turned and saw the doctor's secretary hurrying toward them.

"Lady Woodridge." The secretary pressed her hand against her chest. "I'm glad I caught up with you. The doctor wishes to have a word with you."

Evie and Tom exchanged a look of surprise but wasted no time in following the secretary back to the doctor's surgery.

～

Moments later, they walked into the surgery and were invited to sit down.

"Young lady, you have piqued my curiosity. It's not often that happens. I am due to visit a patient soon, so I will try to be as brief as I can be. Part of the examination I performed included checking for broken bones." He shook his head. "You'd be surprised what some people are capable of doing. I've heard of a farmer breaking a leg bone, dragging himself back home and thinking he could fix it all with a good night's rest. Some people have no idea what they can set into motion. Anyhow, I checked for broken bones and that included the chest." He leaned forward and pulled out a book from a stack on his desk. Searching through it, he found the page he wanted and tapped a finger on it.

Evie and Tom studied the image. It was of a skeleton.

The doctor pointed to the chest. "When a person suffers a heart attack, a doctor performs what is known as chest compressions. It's been in practice since the late 1800s. The effort to start the heart pumping again can cause ribs to crack." He sat back and studied Evie. Seeing no obvious sign of distress, he continued, "There is a case from that same time period of two men inducing death by pressing against the chest and covering the nose and mouth so their victim struggled to draw breath. They were in the business of inducing death without leaving any discernable marks, all in order to harvest the bodies for autopsies and, of course, monetary gain. For a brief time, this was quite a lucrative business. The short of it is, if you lean on a person's chest long enough to prevent them from drawing breath and block their nose and mouth, they will eventually asphyxiate."

"And now you're going to tell me you found no signs of damaged ribs," Evie said.

"That is correct. However… there is a way of putting pressure on the chest without breaking the ribs."

"May I ask why you felt compelled to share that information?"

"For my own peace of mind, of course. Regardless of what you might think, I believe I performed my duty. However, that is not to say I am infallible. I might have missed something." He lifted a finger as if in warning. "And I'm only now thinking about it."

Because she had questioned him?

"In other words, where there is a will there is definitely a way. If you are still in doubt about Enid Carlton's cause of death, then I suggest you try to convince the authorities to look into it. I should be quite happy to provide what input I can. If need be, I will own up to entertaining a few doubts."

He was, of course, referring to an exhumation.

Would it come to that?

"Dr. Mason, that is very accommodating of you."

They left his office with renewed enthusiasm.

"Before you say it, I am eating humble pie. Dr. Mason has actually left me in awe of his talents."

CHAPTER 15

The small village did not have a police presence. However, the publican directed them to the nearest constabulary which proved to be an exercise in futility.

While the policeman in charge took down the information, he did not ask any pertinent questions. Nor did he express any surprise at what they told him. Evie found his manner annoyingly distant even as she tried to excuse his attitude with a degree of empathy.

It had to be difficult for someone to deal with criminal activities on a daily basis. They would either need to grow a thick skin or remain thoroughly impervious.

"Countess, you are to be commended. I thought you might hit him over the head with your handbag."

"It seems we are the only ones concerned with this." Evie gave a firm nod. "That should be enough, for now, at least."

"Someone has to care?" Tom asked.

"Indeed."

As Tom held the motor car door open for her, Evie drew in a breath and stepped in. "We have our suspicions further enhanced by the coincidental death of at least one other graduate from the academy," Evie said. "Dare we risk contacting the authorities now? Will they take us seriously?"

"I take it you are dismissing our efforts with the local constabulary."

"Well, wouldn't you? You saw how our information was received. I'm surprised we were not issued with a warning to stay out of police business."

Tom nodded. "Are you now prepared to consider it more practical and sensible to approach someone we know?"

Detective Inspector O'Neil or Detective Inspector Evans?

Evie knew they had some influence over both detectives. With Caro's help, of course, they might actually have more swaying power over Lord Evans.

However, after recent events, she wished to give Lady Evans some breathing space.

"Perhaps it might be best if we return to the castle. We could place a telephone call from there." And, Evie thought, the time it would take to drive back could be used to decide their next step.

She could not, in all good conscience, storm into Allenford Castle and accuse Lord and Lady Moorsley's guests of murder.

And yet…

Evie felt sure someone in the group of guests had played a role in Enid Carlton's demise.

She sat back and thought about the two other deaths which might be linked to this one.

They couldn't be dismissed as random or coincidental. While they didn't know how the other two women had died, the fact remained, they had been associated with Bramswood Academy.

Tom nodded. "Back to the castle."

As he drove out of the village, Evie settled back and decided to focus on motive.

"Assuming we are on the right track, someone stood to gain something by Enid's death."

Tom gripped his hands around the steering wheel. "You're suggesting someone might have gone to great lengths to gain something or keep something."

"Silence is the ultimate prize. People have been known to kill to secure it and, yes, I am now proposing the idea of Enid being privy to certain information." Evie closed her eyes. "I can't really explain my reasoning other than to say it has something to do with secrets and the sisterhood."

"That's perfectly fine, Countess. You don't have to explain yourself to me. Somehow, everything always falls into place." He tapped his finger on the steering wheel. "Just so you know, I'm not taking anything to my grave. I most certainly don't wish to be killed for something I might or might not know."

What did they know about the Bramswood Academy graduates? Only that they all aspired to something greater. They were taught to avoid settling for second-best. How far would they go to attain their goals?

"Eleanor Stevens."

Tom glanced at her. "Did you say something?"

"I'm thinking about something Horacia said. Only but the deepest love will persuade her into matrimony."

"She obviously hasn't met the right man yet."

"Actually, Horacia was speaking in reference to Eleanor Stevens. She doesn't believe it's a love match."

"That's not unusual among your set."

Evie's voice hitched. "My set? You seem to be excluding yourself."

Tom smiled at her. "You know what I mean."

"I'm not sure that I do. As far as I'm concerned, you belong to my set."

Tom gave her a worried look. "I'm suddenly thinking about sow's ears and silk purses."

"What nonsense. Everyone in my orbit belongs to my set. You know very well I do not discriminate. In any case, you have lovely ears."

Tom shook his head. "It's those curve balls that I have to watch out for."

Evie remembered the letters she had sent Lotte and Millicent. They wouldn't receive them until the next day or, possibly, later.

She could do with Lotte's advice and Millicent's research would serve as confirmation.

With two other deaths related to Bramswood Academy, they could no longer think of this as a coincidence. Evie believed Detective Inspector O'Neil would agree with her.

"Anyhow, what were we saying?"

"You were talking about Eleanor Stevens and her lack of love."

"Oh, yes. Then Horacia said Eleanor had deceived them all. Apparently, she's quite the free-spirit and wishes to live in cosmopolitan cities but she is now pretending to want to settle down to a quiet life in the country."

Tom slowed down and leaned toward her. "So you think she would be willing to kill for the sake of keeping her secret and going ahead with her ruse?"

Did she? It seemed rather extreme.

Then again, what did they know about Eleanor Stevens' circumstances?

"She would be mad to do so." There had to be a greater threat to her plans for happiness. "Apparently, she is a perfect candidate, hailing from the right family and so on. What if there's a secret she doesn't wish her fiancé to know about, certainly not until it's too late?"

How could they delve into her background without appearing too obvious about it?

Would Horacia Deblin assist them? They would have to share what they knew with her.

What if she closed ranks and put more value on protecting the sisterhood?

"Do we know when Eleanor arrived at Allenford Castle?" Tom asked.

Retracing her activities was something the police would know how to tackle.

"You're thinking about opportunity."

Tom nodded. "These deaths happened as a lead up to her arrival at the castle."

Evie tried to picture the young woman taking care of business before she headed to the castle for a few days of fishing.

She had appeared to be quite calm. Did that make her capable of carrying out her acts of violence?

To what end?

What could she possibly have to gain?

Evie remembered the missing photograph. What if its absence had not been accidental. Yes, Alice Breer might have misplaced it. Or, someone might have taken it.

"What about Beatrice Hammond?"

Evie smiled at him. "Something tells me you would love it if she turned out to be bad person."

Tom scowled. "There's an air of wickedness about her and where there is wickedness there is the possibility of evil."

"Well, she is the complete opposite to Eleanor. Beatrice Hammond had been willing to settle. Now, she wishes to lead a life full of adventure."

"She should become a lady detective," Tom suggested.

Beatrice had said she had someone in mind. Would she be honest about her desires or would she focus on securing what some people thought of as a meal ticket?

Smiling, Evie thought Beatrice was brash enough to make demands and she had no doubt she would succeed at attaining everything she wished for.

Tilting her head, she couldn't help playing around with the idea of extreme actions.

How far would Beatrice go to get what she wanted?

~

Evie sensed the motor car slowing down and only then realized she had dozed off.

Straightening, she looked at Tom and offered an apology. "It seems you are doing all the work while I just sat back and enjoyed a rest."

"Such is my lot in life, Countess. I'm not complaining."

"Why are you stopping here?"

"I thought you might want to discuss our next move. The road to the castle is just up ahead."

"Excellent idea, Tom." If only she had a plan.

"It just occurred to me..." Tom shrugged. "Ada Hodge might actually be a target."

Evie's eyebrows shot up. "Heavens, you're right." A sense of urgency swept through her, followed by guilt. They had been entertaining their suspicions and had driven off without any thought given to those left behind.

"That's actually as far as I went with the idea," Tom said. "In other words, I haven't considered the reasons why she might be a target."

Evie wondered if strongarm tactics would work on Ada. Could they use the threat of repercussions? Evie laughed.

"I must have missed the punchline," Tom said.

Rubbing her eyes, Evie said, "I just considered threatening Ada with repercussions. So much for my bright idea. I can't think of any."

"If she doesn't cooperate with us, her life could be at greater risk," Tom suggested.

Evie agreed with a firm nod. "Fear it is then. What about suspects?"

"You've mentioned Eleanor Stevens and I should like to add Beatrice Hammond."

"Why am I not surprised." Evie rolled her eyes.

"What?" Tom crossed his arms and scowled. "She must surely be guilty of something. Think about it. She has employed a most cunning disguise. In fact, for that reason alone, I would focus on Beatrice."

Before Evie could argue against such a silly idea, she caught a glint of amusement in Tom's eye. "I see, you're teasing me. Does that mean you find my other ideas equally ludicrous?"

"Not at all. Besides, I'm the only one proposing a ludicrous."

She could always trust him to lighten the moment before they became bogged down by the seriousness of the matter.

Evie brushed her hands across her thighs. "Do you think it would be safe to approach Horacia Deblin?" Before he could answer, Evie gasped. "I just remembered something. I mentioned Enid Carlton's name and was disappointed when she didn't immediately recognize it. The academy's secretary can't have done a very good job of letting everyone know about Enid."

"Should that be a person of interest?" Tom asked.

"The secretary?"

He nodded. "Remember, no one actually attended the service. It's possible the secretary did not do her job properly because it didn't suit her purposes."

Of covering her trail? "That actually makes sense. However, targeting her for questioning will mean leaving Allenford Castle. What if the killer is present and has, somehow, been alerted about our visit to Enid's village?"

"A killer with a spy network," Tom mused.

Evie reached across and curled her fingers on his wrist. "Let's just go to the castle and play it by ear."

He drew in a deep breath and nodded. Putting the motor into gear, he approached the road leading to the castle. "Are you sure?"

"Positive."

CHAPTER 16

The moment the castle came into view, every single thought Evie had entertained swept through her. Before she could dismiss all her suspicions as ludicrous, she said, "I don't see anyone out and about."

"We might be too late and they have all been murdered," Tom suggested. As he sped along the drive, he said, "Countess, remember what Dr. Mason said."

He had offered his full support and that served as a reminder. "We should head to the library. I'm sure there's a telephone there."

Tom parked the motor car and they made their way inside. Halfway along the hall, they walked past the billiard room where several men stood around watching a game, their voices muted as they focused on a shot.

"It seems they have found something to entertain themselves with."

Hurrying toward the library, they stopped at the door and eased it open a fraction.

"The coast is clear. There's no one here."

"Would you like me to stay by the door while you place the call? Just in case someone comes in."

Evie nodded and searched for the telephone. She found it right where she expected it to be, on the large mahogany desk near a window.

She dug inside her handbag and retrieved her little black book where she kept her contact details.

With any luck, she'd be put through to the detective and she'd find him in a receptive mood.

"Lady Woodridge."

To her surprise, Detective Inspector O'Neil spared her the usual pleasantries.

"How can I help you?"

In a moment of panic, Evie forgot everything she had planned on saying and blurted out, "You could come down to Allenford Castle straightaway."

~

Evie tipped her head back and closed her eyes. After providing details of their location, the detective had explained the logistics of traveling from town up to the Peak District.

To Evie's surprise, he had then proceeded to ask if they had secured the murder weapon.

Evie had laughed. Of course, with her help, he had jumped to conclusions.

"It would take too long to explain."

He had promised to do what he could and, since no murder appeared to have been committed, he had recommended staying out of sight of any and all possible murder suspects.

Evie groaned. "I can't tell if he was humoring me."

The door to the library opened and the butler, Simmons, stepped in carrying a tray with refreshments.

Tom hurried to meet him and explained, "Lady Woodridge is feeling much better but I think it would be best if we have some quiet for a while longer."

Simmons nodded and retreated from the library. However, before he closed the door, Tom asked, "Has anything happened during our absence?"

"Nothing but a mild upheaval in the kitchen. No one expected the guests to cancel their fishing outing and return for luncheon. The ladies are in the drawing room and the gentlemen are engaged in a billiards tournament."

"And what about Lady Constance and her friends?"

"They are under house arrest, not permitted to set foot outside the castle for the duration of their stay."

It seemed the Brigadier had set his foot down.

Tom thanked him and brought the tray in, setting it beside Evie.

"Did you have to make it sound so dramatic?" Evie asked.

"It was all I could think of saying to stop him from

letting everyone know we were here. This way, we can be sure to have the library to ourselves."

"My brain has come to a full stop. I can't begin to imagine what the detective will do. Honestly, Tom, I rely on you to be my voice of reason." Evie rolled her eyes. "My apologies. I don't mean to lay this at your feet. I should have realized it would be impractical for the detective to fly here at the drop of a hat."

Tom poured tea into a cup and handed it to Evie. "Can you just picture it? Someday, in the not so distant future, we might be able to jump on an airplane and cover unimaginable distances in a fraction of the time."

Evie tried to picture it but failed miserably.

As she sipped her tea, she considered placing another telephone call. This time, to Halton House.

"That's silly," Evie muttered. "It would take far too long to explain things to Millicent."

"Are you arguing with yourself?" Tom asked.

"Yes, and doing a very bad job of it." She set her teacup down and stood up. "I suppose we should set out to mingle with the guests and see if we can discover anything new. I trust the detective will come up with a feasible solution. Oh... oh, dear. I've just realized he will most likely contact a local detective. Think of it, Tom. We'll have to impress someone new."

Tom smiled. "The horror." Shaking his head, he assured her, "Take heart, the detective will, no doubt, put in a good word for you."

"I suppose I should try to organize my thoughts. If I'm right and he does send another detective, we will have to explain everything from the very beginning." Her shoulders rose and fell. "Then again, we could take the initiative, go out there and confront everyone with our suspicions."

"That would be an interesting exercise. If the guilty party is present, they might be driven to do something extremely foolish. My money is still on Beatrice Hammond."

They both heard the door opening and turned to find Horacia Deblin standing there.

Evie and Tom exchanged a look that spoke of doubt. Could they trust her?

"Here you are. I thought I saw your motor car driving in."

Evie pushed out a breath and decided to risk it. "Horacia. Do you remember me asking if you knew Enid Carlton?"

The edge of her lip lifted. Horacia nodded. "Yes, poor Enid."

Evie's lips parted. "You remember her." Or had she recognized the name all along?

Horacia laughed. "You can't seriously expect me to remember the names of every pupil."

So… she didn't remember her?

"Yes, fine… I do admit to recognizing the name." Horacia walked along the bookcases, stopping every few paces to read a title before moving on. "There is a protocol in place at Bramswood Academy. We are all encouraged to keep track of marriages, births and deaths. As I said, we think of ourselves as the sisterhood. It would be rude not to take an interest."

"Did you contact the Bramswood Academy secretary?"

Horacia stilled. She had her back to them so Evie couldn't read her expression but she thought she detected a hint of tension on her shoulders.

"Indeed, that was my first idea."

"And?"

"And then I realized I could find the answer right under my nose."

That sounded promising. Evie's gaze shifted to Tom. He stood a few paces away from Horacia, his hands clasped behind his back, his brows drawn down.

He met Evie's gaze but did not change his expression of intense focus. Had something caught his interest?

Horacia appeared to be biding her time. Almost as if she wished to weave a tale.

Turning to face them, Horacia leaned against a bookshelf. "Over the years, you get to hear so many stories about so and so doing this, marrying or starting a family. We've only had a couple of deaths. And... suddenly, there are more than a couple. It's enough to make one wonder."

Evie was beginning to find Horacia's tone slightly worrying. She'd heard it several times before, always employed by someone lamenting their fate or excusing their behavior. To her surprise, she only now realized the guilty... the killers always sounded as if they were just beyond reach, hovering between the here and now and their inner most thoughts.

"I knew Enid Carlton," Horacia finally revealed. She went on to describe her as vivacious and quite engaging. The fact you were asking about her set alarm bells ringing. What could the Countess of Woodridge want with Enid? I could only think of one explanation but it seemed impossible that something might have happened to her. I just didn't wish to believe it. So I asked the Bramswood Academy secretary."

A moment ago, Horacia had said the information had been right under her nose. What had she meant by that? Was the secretary present at Allenford Castle?

The door to the library opened and Simmons walked in. "Lady Woodridge."

"Yes, what is it, Simmons?"

"There is a gentleman who wishes to speak with you."

"Did he give you his name?"

Simmons nodded. "It's Detective Inspector Hollins."

Evie nodded. "Please show him through." Evie and Tom turned toward the library doors.

Just as they opened wider and a man stepped inside, Evie looked over her shoulder.

She expected to find Horacia still standing by the bookshelves. But she was nowhere to be seen.

Swinging around, her eyes rushed to the French doors and she managed to catch sight of her, disappearing around a corner.

Evie stepped forward, her intention to follow her out, when something caught her eye.

Right on the bookshelf where Horacia had been standing a moment before, she saw a small card. Even from where she stood, she recognized it as a calling card.

With her gaze fixed on it, she walked toward it and picked it up.

It seemed like an eternity before her eyes could focus on the slanted lettering.

She read the name and then she read the name again. Then, she looked at the shelf again.

Horacia had left something else. Evie picked it up and studied it closely.

Behind her, she heard Tom introduce himself to the detective. "And this is Lady Woodridge. I take it Detective Inspector O'Neil explained the situation to you."

"He provided an outline. He said you would both offer clarity and that I should pay close attention."

Evie tapped her finger against the card. Turning, she held her hand out.

The detective stepped forward and took it from her hand. Reading it, he then looked up. "Is this a person of interest?"

"You could say that." Evie gave him a brief explanation about Enid Carlton and Alice Breer. "The maid contacted the academy to let them know of Enid's passing. She was assured the information would be shared among the pupils and Enid's friends. However... we have reason to believe the secretary withheld the information and simply took care to send some flowers for the service."

"So... I need to speak with this person," the detective said.

"Yes, you should. I believe you will find her in the drawing room. Although, it might be best to speak with her here. Perhaps we can call for Simmons to organize it."

The detective nodded and, reaching inside his coat, he drew out a notebook. "But first, I would appreciate some more information."

"Certainly, we'll do the best we can."

The detective sat down, his pen poised and ready to take notes.

Evie held up her hand and studied the images on the photograph.

Seeing this, Tom walked toward her. "Evie? What is it?"

She showed him the photograph. "I assume this is what Alice Breer had been looking for. The missing photograph. The killer must have taken it. Either because it provided a trail back to her or because it holds sentimental value."

It also provided proof that the killer had visited Enid Carlton. If she denied it, she would have to explain how it had come to be in her possession.

CHAPTER 17

*H*alf an hour later, Evie felt she and Tom had told the detective everything they knew. None of it could be verified until the detective spoke with the person responsible for killing Enid Carlton.

The matter now rested with him.

They left him to undertake the task and walked out into the afternoon sunshine.

"I can't say I'm pleased about this," Tom said. "I had been counting on Beatrice Hammond's guilt."

His effort to lighten the mood was lost on Evie. Holding her hand up to shield her eyes, she searched the grounds. "There she is, by that tree."

She took a step forward only to stop. "Can you believe it? I mean… All you did was assume I wanted to stop by the village churchyard. And… then, all I did was notice a bunch of flowers."

Tom cupped her elbow and they walked up to Horacia.

Horacia Deblin stood leaning against a tree, her head tipped back, her eyes closed.

If she heard their approach, she did not show it.

She wore a pair of wide-legged trousers, a tweed coat and a beret of the same fabric as the coat.

Her hands were thrust inside the coat pockets and a cigarette dangled from the corner of her mouth.

"Enid Carlton," Horatia said. "I suppose it's only fair to tell you… When you mentioned her name, I recognized it straightaway." She reached for her cigarette, removed it from her mouth and studied it.

"Why didn't you say something?" Evie asked.

"The sisterhood." Horacia shrugged. "I owed it to them to ask around."

"And?"

"Some people knew her better than I did. I confess, I only met her the one time. We were both visiting the academy." She waved her hand as if to dismiss any further explanations as irrelevant. "It might have been an anniversary of sorts. I don't recall." Horacia shrugged. "As far as I could see, if you were interested in her, then something must have happened to her. If that was the case, I knew the academy secretary would have been contacted."

And Horacia had known straightaway the identity of the secretary.

Eleanor Stevens.

"How could you be sure?" Evie shook her head. "I mean, Eleanor might have passed on the information."

Horacia smiled. "To the killer? Possibly. However… I have an inquisitive mind so I delved."

And that's when she'd found the photograph, hidden inside Eleanor's luggage.

Evie had to ask but she feared she already knew the answer. "Who's the man in the photograph?"

"That is or was Eleanor's fiancé. I doubt that marriage will go ahead."

And that, Evie knew, was an understatement. "From what we understand, Enid was rather keen on him."

"It seems quite a few women were keen on him."

Oh, heavens.

Evie looked at Tom. "That explains the trail of deaths."

She turned in time to see Horacia's raised eyebrows.

"There are others?" Horacia asked.

"Two others that we know of. Both graduates of the academy. Either the police will get a full confession out of Eleanor or they will be able to make the connection."

It seemed Eleanor had been eager to clear the way for her marriage to go ahead without any impediment.

Tom shook his head. "For a while there, we thought Ada Hodge might have been a target too, but she's too young to have been involved with him."

The flowers, Evie thought. They must have meant something to her.

She asked Horacia about them.

At first, she shrugged. Then, she pointed toward the house.

Tom and Evie turned and saw Ada Hodge rushing out.

When she reached them, she demanded, "Is it true? Is Eleanor being arrested?"

"It would appear so," Horacia said.

Instead of looking distressed, Ada relaxed.

"Would you care to explain yourself?" Tom asked.

She did, but with the greatest reluctance. "I was at the academy and overheard Eleanor make the arrangements for the flowers to be sent. I found it odd, so I asked her about it. I've never seen her so angry. She made me promise I wouldn't mention it. When I arrived at Allenford Castle and saw them on display I just knew she wanted to send me a warning. I told the others. That's when they came up with the prank to float the flowers down the river. Of course, Eleanor didn't find it at all amusing."

Evie swung away and looked toward the river.

All this had been about clearing the way for a comfortable future of privilege and status. How could she have ever lived with herself, knowing her wishes had cost the lives of others?

Evie couldn't help asking, "What do you think Anita May Connors will have to say about this?"

"I doubt she'll spend any time dwelling. We'll close ranks and shield her from the worst of it."

But Eleanor would be on her own.

≈

Shortly after...

Reluctant to linger, Tom and Evie loaded their luggage and headed back to Halton House.

"Rose is waving," Tom said.

As she turned, Evie asked, "Is she holding up two hats? I might have left them behind."

"I think you're safe to wave. Actually, I'm surprised she's not coming along with us."

"Well, it seems I'm the one who made her nervous. She'd heard a few tales about me and feared I was there to investigate."

Tom grinned. "You might want to change your mind about her. She could come in handy."

Evie rolled her eyes and asked, "What are we going to tell the others? They won't be at all pleased to have missed out on the excitement."

Tom studied her for a moment. Lifting the edge of his lip, he stretched his hands out and said, "That you caught the biggest fish in the river. Then again, don't you want your moment in the sun? You read the signs from the start. At the very least, you'll have to tell Lotte Mannering. This will surely impress her."

"I'm not sure about that. Maybe I just want to focus on smaller fish."

"Well, if you won't tell her..."

Evie employed her warning tone, "Tom, don't you

dare spread rumors about me. At least not until we're well clear of Allenford Castle. You know, the tales here are quite tall."

***

Printed in Great Britain
by Amazon

49307629R00101